THE WITCH WAR

OF FIDDLEHEAD CREEK

THE COMPLICATED LIFE OF DEEGIE TIBBS BOOK II

C. L. HERNANDEZ

PERMUTED
PRESS

A PERMUTED PRESS BOOK
ISBN: 978-1-68261-596-6

The Witch War of Fiddlehead Creek:
The Complicated Life of Deegie Tibbs Book II

Permuted Press, LLC
New York • Nashville
permutedpress.com
Published in the United States of America

For Olivia Marie, my greatest blessing

PROLOGUE

Roland chased the vague form of Tiger Spirit through the soot-blackened maze of corridors and tunnels until the mighty beast could run no more. He hovered, flickering in and out of shape behind the steaming boulders at the end of a long-unused storage alcove. Only his eyes, slit-pupiled and blazing amber, remained sharply delineated. Roland still heard the faint racket of the foot soldiers echoing through the vast caverns of the Underworld. His men were deeply involved in the reappearance of the demon Chul, finally home after a long imprisonment on the Earthly Plane; none of them had followed him. He gave a final glance around, and then, with careful footsteps, he approached the weak and ragged Spirit Animal.

"Hello, old friend." Roland knelt a few yards from Tiger Spirit, extended a hand, and made gentle beckoning gestures. "You're safe here. Let me help you."

Weakened as he was by the battle with Chul, Tiger still managed a deafening warning bellow, and he slashed at the air with a mighty paw. Roland saw no hint of recognition in the glowing lanterns of Tiger's eyes. He backed away, breaking eye contact and keeping his motions cautious and unhurried. Tiger Spirit was in shreds, weakened to the point of vanishing forever, but still deadly. Roland lowered his voice and tried again.

"It's been a long time since I saw you last. I remember the night I conjured you from the spirit world as a guardian for my daughter."

Tiger flickered orange and black, and his answering growl made the smoking ground shiver under Roland's feet.

"Back then you knew me as Roland Tibbs, but down here I am called Klaa. And my daughter is Deegie."

At the sound of his mistress's name, Tiger Spirit collapsed on the pebbled ground and disappeared. Only his eyes remained visible, and they were glassy and huge. Ragged, high-pitched growls, sounding eerily like human sobbing, tore from the noble spirit animal and echoed down the deserted chambers.

"You *do* know me," Roland said. "Now you remember, don't you?"

Spirit animals are not capable of speech, but Roland knew Tiger understood. "Easy now," he said, and he went to the creature's side again and sat beside him. He placed his hands on Tiger's head, carefully, one at a time, and then closed his eyes. "Be still. I will help you."

Roland went silent and still, his fingers buried in Tiger's thick, unseen pelt. His body began to tremble, minutely at first, then increasing as he transferred energy from his body into that of the huge feline Spirit Guardian. Tiger's agonized growls quieted and finally ceased. A purring sound, deep and rumbling, echoed off the stone walls of the Underworld chamber as the great beast absorbed Roland's life-saving gift.

"There you are," Roland said after the transfer was complete. His forehead sparkled with the sweat of his efforts; in the dim red light of the Underworld it looked like blood. "Just rest now. You will recover. You're safe here. It's not where you're supposed to be, I know, but no further harm will come to you."

Roland could not communicate with Tiger Spirit, not verbally anyway. Back when he had lived on the Earthly Plane, he had been one of the most powerful Dark Witches in the world. Although his human life had been snuffed out by an assassin and his immortal soul banished to the Underworld, he had retained those powers and he utilized one of them now. Returning his hands to Tiger's sleek head, Roland delved into the spirit animal's mind and searched his memories.

Images of Deegie came to him and played out in his own mind, stuttering, jittery, and out of focus. It was like watching a home movie that had been stored in an attic for decades. Deegie's face was blurry and indistinct, but Roland could still see that she had become a very beautiful woman. The images came faster now: Deegie behind the counter in a curio shop of some sort, working an old-fashioned cash register; the close, cluttered interior of an elderly Volkswagen; a jar of shriveled human fingers; then Deegie again, opening the very portal through which Tiger Spirit and the demon Chul were thrust. Distracted and dismayed, Roland broke the connection. He had not expected this, but at the same time, he wasn't surprised; Deegie had always been rebellious.

Oh shit, what has she done? Roland shrouded his face with his hands. *I should never have taught her those dark spells, not even the harmless ones. And those damn books! She must have found them and read every single one!*

The books were Roland's own, an entire shelf full of magical grimoires that had always been strictly off-limits to his precocious young daughter. He should have thrown them away; he should have burned them. His courier, Hack, provided him with updates every month after delivering her monthly inheritance money. Until now, Roland had been convinced that his only daughter was safe and healthy. By opening a portal to the Underworld, an act expressly forbidden to all but the most experienced of Dark Witches, Deegie had put herself in mortal danger. The assassin who had torn Roland's family apart and left young Deegie an orphan was an old man now, but as far as Roland knew, he was still alive. If he found out what Deegie had done, he would be only too glad to renew his search for the last remaining member of the Tibbs family. And now Deegie was without her guardian.

3

CHAPTER ONE

January sunshine filtered through the bay window of the living room in the old house on Fox Lane. Deegie Tibbs stood in that square of golden warmth, watching the drip and gleam of the icicles hanging from the eaves. The TV droned on behind her, the morning news finally switching topics. Deegie scolded herself for turning it on in the first place; there was always something to stress out about when one watched the news. She swiped at the condensation on the window and dried her wet palm on her skirt. After a final glance at the forested hill behind her house, she closed the curtains. Something stalked that dense pine forest, something with teeth and claws and murderous intent. The last thing she wanted was to see it peering through her window.

The folks at KXLY-TV were calling it a bear now; yesterday they were convinced it was a large feral dog. Witnesses stated they had seen a hulking, shaggy, four-legged *something*. Enormous, misshapen paw prints were found in the snow, the tracks looping and circling in random patterns before disappearing back into the woods. Worst of all were the missing pets. Deegie could not bear to think about this part for long. Losing a beloved animal companion was as agonizing as losing a human family member. Impulsively, she went to the couch and scooped up Bast, the black kitten she'd rescued from a dumpster, and she cuddled him in her arms. Bast looked up at her quizzically, as if he was wondering what she had done with the sunlight he'd been enjoying.

Snuggling with Bast naturally brought on thoughts of Tiger, her lost guardian spirit animal. She missed him more than ever now and hoped he hadn't suffered when he was dragged into the Underworld. She yearned for one of his surprise visits and ached to hear his grunted feline greetings. Life without him was still strange, and she felt vulnerable and exposed. She dreamed of him nearly every night.

"Don't worry, Bast," she said, as if the kitten could understand her. "I won't let anything happen to you. Ready to go to work?" Deegie sniffled and brought a hand to her throat. Either she had a nose full of kitten hair, or she was coming down with something. She put Bast in his carrier, snapped off the TV, and picked up her coat and purse. After standing in the open doorway and cautiously surveying her surroundings, she hurried across the snowy yard to her car, clambered in and headed down the icy street. Moley was meeting her today before work to deliver her monthly inheritance money. Weird, smelly, hunched-over Moley was the last thing she wanted to see, but money was always a welcome sight. *Mr. Hack,* she corrected herself, *his name is Mr. Hack, not Moley.* It was hard not to think of him as Moley, though. He looked just like a human/mole hybrid.

The line at the corner store was long, and Zach Altman's patience was growing short. *Must be a new cashier,* he thought, watching the harried young blonde woman at the register. *Jeez, hurry it up a little, lady! I'd like to pay for my gas and raisin Danish before the next election, if possible!*

As if the line weren't bad enough, Zach's brother, Gilbert, was relieving his own frustration by surreptitiously sending out invisible pulses of energy to move, rattle, and knock over random items in the crowded convenience store. With a brisk snap of his fingers, he set a cardboard beer promo into motion. It swayed back and forth on the strings that suspended it from the ceiling. Then Gilbert nodded his head at the plastic bins of beef jerky sitting on the counter next to the register. The dried strips of meat began dancing and whirling in their see-through cubicles. *Snap!* went Gilbert's fingers again, and a row of bagged popcorn fell gracefully, one after the other, from their display. A synchronized swimming team couldn't have done better.

"What, we havin' an earthquake or somethin' now on top of everything else?" a fat man in sweatpants asked as his eyes tracked the swaying beer sign.

"It's just the heater kicking on, I'm sure," Zach said. "See the vents up there?"

The fat man glared at him wordlessly and went back to gazing at the snack cakes.

Zach heard gasps and surprised exclamations coming from the head of the line now; the dancing jerky strips had been noticed as well.

Snap! A bag of jellybeans slid off its peg and fell to the floor. It scribed a perfect circle on the worn linoleum, then split itself open and spilled multi-colored candies in all directions.

"Gilbert, knock it off!" Zach hissed under his breath.

Gilbert smirked. "Just trying to keep myself entertained."

Zach cringed. If it hadn't been for his empty gas tank, he would have ditched the raisin Danish and hustled his mischievous brother out of there. Being the only Normal One in a family of witches certainly had its trying moments.

The fat man cupped a hand around his mouth and hollered at the cashier. "Hey! Hurry it up, will ya?"

"Hey look, there's Deegie." Gilbert nudged his older brother and pointed toward the window.

Zach looked. Yep, that was Deegie all right; he'd recognize that unruly black hair anywhere. She stood in front of the post office across the street, her hands full of mail, having a discussion of some sort with an odd-looking man in a black hat and sunglasses.

"Who the hell is that?" Gilbert narrowed his eyes as he peered at Deegie and the stranger.

"Hell, I dunno. Some old guy."

"That was a rhetorical question," Gilbert snorted derisively. "That means it doesn't require an answer."

"I know that, Gilbert!"

Zach was curious himself and continued to watch. The stranger handed Deegie a thick envelope that she hastily tucked into her purse, then he bowed theatrically, turned, and headed off down the sidewalk in the opposite direction.

Must have had some of her mail, Zach concluded. When he turned his head away from the window, he saw, much to his great relief, that the convenience store's manager had taken over the register, and the line was finally moving.

"I can't believe Deegie still wants to live in that house," Gilbert remarked once they were back in the truck and headed for work. "Demons in the basement, ghosts in the attic, dead hobos in the woods, and now something's roaming around killing house pets and scaring the crap out of people. She's either very brave or very stupid."

"Don't call Deegie stupid!" Zach snapped. He was still highly annoyed with his brother over the stunts he'd pulled at the store. He guided the truck into its parking spot behind Altman Heating and Air and cut the engine. "Deegie's incredibly brave, very stubborn, and, yeah, a little bit weird, but she's *not* stupid!"

"Damn, but you're touchy today! Did someone piss in your cereal or something?"

Zach ignored his brother's comment and fitted his work cap over his red hair. "Come on," he said. "Let's get this over with."

Deegie gazed at the pile of boxes on the floor of the back room at The Silent Cat: the delivery from yesterday still hadn't been put away. She sniffled again and winced at the prickly sensation in her throat. *I'm not getting sick,* she insisted to herself. *Nope, not me. Not sick at all.* She counted the money in the envelope that Moley had given her before she did anything else. Despite her discomfort, she managed a smile. Thanks to her monthly inheritance money, she was growing ever closer to her dream of opening a shelter for stray cats. She put the money back in her purse and let Bast out of his carrier.

She switched on the hot plate behind the counter and filled the teakettle. Then, reminding herself that she wasn't getting sick, she selected jars of elder, peppermint, and yarrow from the herb shelves. Maybe a medicinal tea would head off the cold she wasn't getting. Sipping tea as she worked, Deegie unpacked boxes of oils and gemstone nuggets, along with bags of fresh herbs, and a cardboard display of colorful woven bracelets for the counter.

The last box held an antique talking board, a device similar to a Ouija Board. It supposedly allowed the operator to communicate with the spirit world. She'd seen it online, and though it was a bit on the expensive side, she couldn't resist. Made of wood, it was in the shape of a half-moon with the letters of the alphabet painted on in flowy gold-leaf script. The paint was still bright, and there were only a few chips. It was missing its planchette, the device the spirits used to spell out their messages, but it was still a stunning piece of art. She decided to use it as part of the shop's décor. It would look great hanging on the wall above the register.

On the other side of the closed blinds, a vehicle pulled into the parking lot. She heard a car door slam, then determined footsteps marched through the slush, heading for the locked front door of The

Silent Cat. Knuckles rapped impatiently on the glass, hard enough to make the SORRY, WE'RE CLOSED sign rattle.

"All right, all right, I'm coming. Hold your horses!" Deegie's voice was ragged and husky as she went to the front of the shop to open for business.

Her first customer of the day was a dark-haired young man who wore a look of utter shock on his face. "You sell magical supplies, right?" His voice carried a sharp edge of panic, and his eyes ticked back and forth as he surveyed the shop's interior.

"Yes, I do," Deegie replied warily. "Is there something I can help you—"

"I need silver bullets!" The man clutched at Deegie's sleeve as he spoke. "That's the only thing that's gonna kill that werewolf in the woods, ya know!"

CHAPTER TWO

Deegie sensed no danger in the frightened-looking young man, but she pulled her arm away from him just the same. "I don't sell silver bullets," she said with honest regret. "Sorry."

"I saw it," he said, his voice a desperate whisper. "I saw that thing last night."

"What thing?" Deegie frowned and took a step backward. "That creature from the news, you mean?"

"Yes! That...that *thing!* It was in my yard last night. The newspeople got it all wrong. It ain't no bear, and it ain't no stray dog! It's a werewolf!" His eyes brimmed and spilled over, and tears coursed down his stubbled cheeks. "I tried to tell the police, but they thought I was a whack-job, I guess." He scrubbed at his wet face with grimy hands. "Lady, I swear to you I'm not drunk or on drugs. I know what I saw."

"Okay, okay. Look, just have a seat over there." She gestured toward the reading nook at the front of the shop, where chilly sunlight spilled through the window. "I'll make you some tea. I'll listen to you."

It wasn't the first time Deegie had soothed the frazzled nerves of someone claiming to have seen monsters, UFOs, and other creepy crawlies. Most of the time, these sightings were the result of too much partying, or an over-active imagination, but not this time. Something had frightened this guy half out of his wits. She hastily prepared a cup of chamomile and valerian tea, refilled her own cup, and went to the round table next to the window.

He introduced himself as Thomas Beyer, and he sat across from her, his hands wrapped around the warm mug. His full-body trembling had ceased, but his expression was still troubled, and bruise-colored half-moons lay under his eyes. Deegie could tell it had been a while since he last slept.

"I'm glad my wife and kids didn't see that thing," he said at last, his voice cracking as he spoke.

"Tell me what you saw." Deegie leaned forward, her cold forgotten for now.

Thomas spread his hands wide, and his breath hitched in his throat. "I saw... it was a werewolf. I know how crazy that sounds, but I know what I saw, and it weren't no bear! They didn't believe me. Them cops didn't believe me at all!"

"*I* believe you," Deegie said. And she did. She believed he'd seen *something*, anyway. The stark terror she felt emanating from him couldn't be anything but genuine. "I know it couldn't have been a bear; don't they hibernate during the winter?"

"Exactly!" Thomas's head bobbed up and down in an enthusiastic nod. "The bears are asleep!" His voice rose and cracked again, hovering on the brink of hysteria.

"Shhh," Deegie pointed at his mug of tea. "Just drink that. You're okay. You're safe."

"It was huge and black," Thomas said. "Four legs, all crooked and weird, like they was broke and didn't heal right." He raked his fingers through his dark hair and squeezed his eyes shut, as if the memory caused him physical pain. "The face... it turned and looked right at me... the mouth was open and the tongue all hanging out. The jaws looked all wrong, too. Crooked, and just... you know, not right."

"Deformed? Is that what you mean?"

"Yeah! Like it was s'posed to be a dog, but didn't quite make it." He uttered an odd, strangled laugh. "Damn cops though I was on drugs."

"Are you?" Deegie cocked a brow at him.

"No, I swear I'm not! I don't mess with that stuff, I told you that! I know what I saw!" He stood and gulped down the rest of his tea, then wiped his mouth with a hand that still trembled. "Thank you for the tea. Don't go into the woods, lady. Whatever you do, don't go into the woods."

Thomas Beyer yanked open the door and returned to his car at a dead run, presumably to resume his search for silver bullets.

"I won't," Deegie said to the empty shop.

As far as Deegie knew, werewolves had died out over a century ago. At least, that's what her father had told her, and she'd never actually seen one. What were the chances that one of the shaggy beasts roamed the thick forest surrounding Fiddlehead Creek?

No, she thought to herself, *no way.* Beyer's description was way off. From the waist down, the long-extinct species were human. They walked upright and had short, flattened snouts. The terrified man's description better fit a stray, malformed dog.

Deegie tried forcing herself to put the matter aside and focus on work, but she wasn't very successful. In her mind, she still saw Thomas Beyer's wet, frightened eyes and heard the desperation in his voice. It was at times like this when she wished she knew more people like herself. The only other witch she knew was Gilbert Altman, Zach's cocky, arrogant brother. She'd have to be hard up for advice before consulting *that* guy. Not that he wasn't knowledgeable—he was, but he made sure everyone else knew it, too.

The front door banged open, and a blonde girl in her late teens entered the shop; Deegie recognized her immediately. Tamara Biggs was the queen of the teen scene in Fiddlehead Creek, the living cliché that all the young men wanted to date and all the less attractive girls wanted to be. Tamara marched up to the counter, her blonde curls bouncing. "I need you to teach me how to cast a love spell on someone," she announced, "and it needs to be fast-acting. How much do you charge for that?"

Deegie managed to stop her upturning gaze before it turned into a full-fledged eye-roll. When one owns a magical supply shop, there is never a shortage of folks who want to cast love spells. She was more than a little surprised, however, that Tamara, in all her enviable blonde glory, would ever need one. Hidden by the counter, Deegie's hands tightened into fists, then relaxed. *Two weirdos back to back when I'm feeling like shit. It's going to be a great day,* she told herself. Aloud, she said, "No can do. Love spells are never a good idea." Her tone was a little harsher than she had intended, so she followed up with a wide, fake smile.

"What do you mean?" Tamara cocked her head to the side and narrowed her overly made-up eyes. "This is a magic shop, and you sell magical stuff, right? Stuff for spells and junk?"

"Well, yes, but let me explain: interfering with another person's free will is—"

"Oh, pffft! A spell is a spell. Don't give me that crap. It's pretty obvious you're not a *real* witch!" Tamara made a dismissive gesture with her hand and picked up the talking board, turning it from side to side as she examined it.

"I never said I was." Deegie frowned and added, "Sorry, that's not for sale. Please put it down."

"What is it? A magical thing?"

"It's called a talking board. It's for communication with spirits." The phone rang then, and Deegie turned to answer it. "Now hang on one sec, and I'll tell you why you shouldn't cast love spells."

But when she finished the call and returned to the counter, the prom queen was gone. And so was the antique talking board.

"Aw, damn it." Deegie slumped in her chair and passed a hand over her hot forehead. Bast stopped licking his paws, gave her a onceover with his golden eyes, and then went back to sleep. "You could have at least—I don't know—scratched her or something," she told him. "Some security guard *you* are!"

By the end of the day, Deegie felt utterly wretched. Friday nights usually involved take-out pizza, microbrews, and a few hands of poker with Zach and Gilbert, but not this time. Nestled under a pile of blankets with Bast and a bottle of NyQuil, she called the Altman brothers' house and was secretly glad when Zach answered the phone. After the horrid day she'd had, she didn't have the patience to talk to Gilbert.

"Hey, Zach." She had to clear her throat several times before she could finish her sentence. "I'm not gonna make it tonight. I have some sort of deadly mystery disease. I'll probably die." Her weak laugh ended in a hearty coughing spell.

"Huh? Is that you, Deeg?" Zach's voice held a note of hesitation, as if he wasn't sure if he should laugh at her joke.

"Yeah, it's me. What's left of me, anyway."

"Damn, you sound *awful!* Do you need me to bring you anything? Juice? Soup? A jar of fingers?"

"Very funny, Altman." She knew his concern was genuine though, and it made her smile. She was quite aware of Zach's crush on her, and there were days when she wondered if she felt the same way. "No, I'll be okay. I have tissues and tea and soup. Sorry I can't make it, though. Guess I'll have to kick your butts at Texas Hold 'Em next week."

"Aw, honey, that's okay. We understand. You just take it easy and get well."

Before she could reply, she heard Gilbert's voice in the background: "Hey, is that Deeg? And what do we understand? Let me talk to her."

After a rustle, a thump, and a muffled exchange between the two brothers, Gilbert was on the line. "Hey," he said, "so you're sick, huh?"

"Yeah, Gil, but I'll be fine, really. I just need to..." A thought occurred to her then, and she interrupted her own sentence. "Hey, what do you know about werewolves?"

"Huh? Werewolves? That's kind of random."

"They're extinct, aren't they?"

Gilbert chuckled into the phone. "Yeah, of course they are! Don't tell me you didn't know *that!*"

Ordinarily, Deegie would have bristled at Gilbert's condescending manner, but all day the image of Thomas Beyer's terrified face had been in her mind. "A man came into the store this morning claiming he saw one last night. He said that's what's been roaming around in the woods; a werewolf. He even asked if I had silver bullets."

Gilbert made an arrogant snorting sound. "Really, Deegie," he said, "you know better than that. Most likely, he was just another crack-pot. This town's full of them. Probably on drugs or something, you know?"

"Yeah. You're right." Deegie yanked a pink tissue from the box on the nightstand and dabbed at her nose with it. "It's just that he seemed so sincere, even though the description he gave me didn't fit. Do you suppose there could be another breed of werewolf? A new species, or something?"

"No, Deeg. The werewolves went extinct a long time ago. Whatever's in the woods, it's not a werewolf. It's most likely a big, ugly dog, like the one me and Zach saw on Thanksgiving, remember?"

She closed her eyes and nodded as she massaged her burning forehead with her free hand. Sure she remembered, but that thing had been running at top speed. Kind of hard to see the details when something's moving that fast.

"Deeg...?"

"Huh? Oh, yeah. You're probably right, Gil. Look, I gotta go, okay? I really feel crappy. See ya." She hung up before Gilbert could say anything else.

Ten minutes later, the swamp-green cold and flu medicine took effect, and Deegie gave in to much-needed sleep. Her dreams took on the surreal quality that often accompanies fevers, and tonight she dreamed she was in her old Volkswagen bus, driving cautiously over the tops of the bookshelves downstairs. Apparently it was a perfectly normal thing to do in Dream Land. The bus's A/C wasn't working—had it ever?—and ribbons of sweat poured down her furrowed brow. The rainbow-painted bus slowed to a lurching chug, and the engine let out a weird, lengthy howl. The bus was old, and it had had its fair share of breakdowns, but it had *never* made a noise like this before. She coasted her dream world vehicle to a stop next to a carnival glass candy dish that sat next to the World Encyclopedia vol. 22, W-Z. The bus hissed and shuddered as all four tires deflated suddenly and simultaneously. The vehicle's interior shrank in on itself, and Deegie wrenched the wheel in frantic arcs, screaming, "I need a map! I need a map!"

Her eyes snapped open; her own yelling voice had awakened her and thrust her back into reality. Bast stood on her bed next to her sweat-soaked pillow with his back arched and his eyes huge. The fur along his spine stood straight up and his tail was fluffed to twice its normal size. He hissed at the window and the darkness beyond it.

Deegie blinked, her expression dazed until she realized where she was. "Bast? Ssh. What's wrong?" She sat up with the sheet puddled in her lap. Her head buzzed and floated. From the snowy ground below the bedroom window rose a howl, thin and wavering—the sound from the dream. Bast dove beneath the bed and tucked himself into a dusty corner. Deegie's feet touched the wooden floor, and she winced at the sudden chill. With her arms wrapped around her shoulders, she shuffled to the bedroom window and peered through the frosty glass.

Next to the recycling bin an enormous creature sat on its haunches, staring up at the moon. The back of its head looked very much like that of a large dog, a Rottweiler or a Doberman perhaps. But when it sensed it was being watched and the black canid head turned in her direction, Deegie saw that this thing was anything but normal. The eyes didn't match; one sat high at the top of the head, the other a few inches lower. They were muddy orange, the same color as the eyes of the demon she had battled not long ago. Insanity shone bright in those off-kilter orbs, and when the creature stood up, it uttered its terrible, piercing howl. Three of its four legs stuck out at impossible angles, bending where no canine leg should bend. The fourth leg looked shriveled and boneless; it flopped uselessly at the creature's side. The thing looked just as the frantic young man had described that morning.

Is this real? Am I still dreaming? She peered hard at the ugly brute in the front yard, and her vision wavered in and out of focus. It was the fever, of course. A hallucination, had to be. Her brain had overheated and reprocessed all her thoughts into some sort of sleepwalk stew. That thing couldn't possibly be real, could it?

Something touched her arm, a feeling like cool mist, and a delicate voice murmured in her ear: *To bed, to bed... illness... please, Miss. To bed.*

She felt herself being tugged along by the sleeve of her nightgown, and Lisbet appeared at her side. Her ghostly face was lined with concern.

"Am I dreaming, Lisbet? I feel so sick."

The ghost did not reply, but Deegie felt a great comfort at her presence. She'd discovered the old lady ghost residing in the house after she'd moved in, and the two of them had formed an immediate bond. Deegie eased herself back under the warm blankets. She felt a quilt being tucked around her shoulders.

Oh, so sick... like 1919... such a flu outbreak. Sleep.

"Yes, back to sleep," Deegie mumbled. Thank all the gods for Lisbet.

The old woman summoned her cats with friendly, nonsensical sounds, and she directed them to Deegie's bed. A baker's dozen of wispy feline ghosts covered the ailing witch in a soft blanket of purring comfort.

Good kitties, Lisbet whispered. *Good babies.*

CHAPTER THREE

When Deegie opened her eyes again, Lisbet and her horde of cats were gone. Strong sunlight lit up the bedroom, and birds hurled avian insults at each other from the branches of the pines. She clamped her lids shut again and covered her eyes with her hand. The sunlight made them sting and water.

"Sorry," Zach said. "I'll close the blinds."

"Huh? Zach?" *What was Zach doing in her bedroom?*

"Yeah, it's me. Don't get up."

She heard the rattle of the blinds being closed and Deegie managed to raise her head from the pillow to look at Zach. "But... how... what day is it?"

"Saturday, around eleven." Zach sat on the edge of the bed and fussed with the blankets, tucking them in around her legs and shoulders. "We kept getting hang-up calls from your cell phone last night, and, well, it was weird enough to warrant a trip over here."

"My phone?" Deegie squinted at her battle-scarred phone, sitting innocently on the nightstand next to her box of tissues. "I never called you guys. And how did you get in? I locked the door. At least I think I did."

"It opened by itself just as we pulled into the driveway, but seeing how it's *your* house, I wasn't really surprised."

Deegie smiled weakly despite her wretchedness. "Lisbet," she said. "I think she was worried about me last night."

"That doesn't surprise me either." Zach leaned over and settled his palm on her forehead. "You're not as hot as you were this morning." Deegie smirked at him. "Seriously, Zach? I'm always hot." Her attempt at humor ended in a coughing spell, and she gave up her usual banter.

"Very funny." He tugged at her blankets again, then settled his hands in his lap. "You're damn sick, Deeg. I'm glad Lisbet called us. Well, she *sorta* called us, anyway."

"I thought it was just a cold, but—ugh. I think I have the flu." She nested her head into the pillow and sniffled. "Hey, where's Gil?"

"He's either setting fire to your kitchen, or making toast. Not sure which."

Gilbert strode into the room as if summoned, balancing a plate of toasted rye bread in one hand and carrying a glass of orange juice in the other. "Deeg, all you had was frozen concentrate. Fresh squeezed really is best when you're sick."

"I'll keep it in mind," Deegie said, rolling her sleepy eyes. But she bit the corner off a piece of toast and drank a swallow of juice just to be polite. "Thanks, you guys, really. I'm going back to sleep now, so lock up when you leave, okay?"

"Yeah, like I'm going anywhere," Zach replied. "You really should let us take you to the hospital or something. The flu can actually kill people."

"I'll be okay," Deegie mumbled into the pillow. She made weak shooing motions at the Altman brothers. "Go on now. Go watch some manly sports on TV or something, and let me die in peace."

But as Zach and Gilbert headed for the door, she remembered something. "Hey wait." She sat up and brushed back her tangled hair. "Remember that guy I told you about who thought he saw a werewolf? Well... there was something outside last night..."

"Deeg, we've been over this already!" Gilbert threw his hands in the air and rolled his eyes heavenward. "Honey, there are *no* werewolves!"

"Knock it off, Gil," Zach chided his brother mildly. "You thought the demon in her basement was no big deal too, and look what happened with that!" He turned, went back to Deegie's bed, and seated himself on the edge. "Tell us what you saw, Deeg."

Gilbert leaned against the door frame and glared at his brother.

"Well," Deegie began, "I was having this crazy dream—you know how dreams get when you're feverish—and there was a howling noise. I thought it was part of the dream, but when I woke up, Bast was all puffed up and scared. I heard the noise again, so I got up to look."

At the sound of his name, Bast stirred in his place by the pillow and opened a sleepy eye. Deegie scooped up the half-grown kitten and nuzzled his head before continuing.

"There was this... this *thing* out in the front yard. At first I thought it was a big dog, but it turned around, like it sensed me, and I saw its face."

"Just a continuation of your dream, most likely," Gilbert muttered from the doorway. "You were probably sleepwalking."

Although she hadn't yet dismissed this possibility, Deegie ignored him and went on. "It had the craziest eyes, reddish-orange. One was way up here, and the other was way down there." She pointed at her own face to demonstrate. "It had three legs, all bent at crazy angles, and one leg was all... weird and shriveled-looking."

"Jeez, Deegie, is *anything* normal in your little world?" Zach smiled at his unusual friend, then eased her back down into her nest of blankets and pillows. "But I think Gil's right. At least this time anyway. You had that crazy guy's creature in your head, and your poor feverish brain had a field day with it."

"Yeah, okay." She felt too tired and sick to discuss it any further. Maybe when she felt better. *Did it even happen in the first place?* She offered the brothers a weak smile. "Going back to sleep now, guys. Don't eat all my food and put the seat down after you pee, 'kay?"

Lisbet hovered out of sight, close to the ceiling, and watched as the two red-haired men tromped down the stairs and into the living room. She'd gotten used to them being here on a regular basis, but she rarely appeared to them when they were around. It had indeed been she who manipulated the phone to contact Deegie's friends. She had been greatly relieved when they had arrived and taken care of poor Deegie, but there was more she needed to convey to them. She'd listened to their conversation, and they were wrong; the creature in the yard last night *was* real. Lisbet had seen it herself, but how to tell them? Even in life, she had had a hard time talking to people.

Oh, my mind! Thinking... not thinking... Words! Words! Bad things again! So bad!

The timid ghost shrank herself into a tiny orb and floated up the staircase to seek comfort in her beloved cats.

Roland sat on a boulder at the very back of the forgotten passage, absently stroking Tiger's great head while he awaited the return of his servant. Hack was always punctual, but still Roland's impatience twisted, worm-like, in his belly. His worry over his daughter was almost unbearable. Every day for a week, he'd slipped away from his duties and visited Tiger Spirit in the abandoned corridor. Tiger was growing strong on Roland's daily energy transfers, and his battle wounds were healing. Soon he would be restored to his former mighty self and be returned to Deegie, where he belonged.

A ripping sound overrode the tranquil stillness of the old corridor, and a narrow portal opened in the rocky wall. Hack slipped through with mincing steps and snatched his black, round-brimmed hat from his head. Tiger rose to his feet, rumbling softly.

"Take it easy." Roland soothed the spirit animal with gentle words and a careful hand. "It's only Mr. Hack, bringing news about our Deegie."

Hack stood before them, hat in hand and waiting to be addressed.

"Good evening, Mr. Hack. What have you learned about my girl?"

Hack offered a barely perceptible bow. "She is safe, sir. A bit ill at the moment, but safe." He tugged at his black overcoat and added, "Sir, would you mind if I switched? This humanoid body is dreadfully uncomfortable, and—"

"Yes, yes, go ahead! Hurry up! I want to hear about my daughter, not your physical discomfort!" Roland curled his fingers into a tight fist, relaxed them, and then sought the comfort of Tiger's fur once more.

Hack's body shimmered, and he released a delighted sigh as his human shape fell away and his true form was revealed. A pink, mole-like demon now stood in front of Roland and Tiger. He scratched eagerly at his butt with his spade-shaped nails and grinned down at his naked groin.

"Hack! Now!"

Roland's voice was as effective as a slap. Hack squealed and saluted. "Yes sir! Your daughter has what is known as the flu on the Earthly Plane. She will recover. There are two men caring for her now."

"Men?" Roland rose from the boulder and touched the hilt of his sword. "What men?"

"Friends, possible suitors. One is a witch, the other a Normal One. Brothers, I think. Not to worry, sir. They are no danger to her." Hack glanced at his nails and licked his lips. "I had a chance to observe one of the assassin's hunters, however. The threat is plausible, but..."

"But *what*, damnit?"

"The assassin Arlo Colbalt is an old man now, sir. His powers are weak, along with his body. Since he can no longer hunt the Dark Ones physically, he conjures hunters and sends them out to search."

Hack sniffed his fingers and chuckled. "The problem is," he went on, "old Arlo has gotten so senile, his creations are little more than failed science projects. He can't create anything with enough brainpower, it seems. The hunters are malformed and stupid; they know they're supposed to be killing something, but they're not sure what. A few house pets have gone missing, but these things are too stupid to go after a human. For now, Deegie is reasonably safe."

Roland was not convinced; reasonable safety was not good enough. When it came to his only child, no threat was too small. *That stupid old man has gone after her now. It was just a matter of time. I'll hunt him down and kill him myself if I have to.* That was the only real decision, as far as he was concerned. He would follow the rules and go before the Underworld Council to beg permission to go to the Earthly Plane. Permission was sometimes granted under certain circumstances, but if they refused him, he would go anyway. He kept that part to himself. The little pink ass-picker in front of him was a good spy, but he didn't need to know everything.

"Very well, Mr. Hack," he said aloud. "You are dismissed."

The mole-demon messenger nodded his pink head. "Absolutely, sir!"

"You are *dismissed*, Hack!"

"Thank you, sir!"

Roland quirked his upper lip in disgust as he watched Hack drop to all fours and scuttle away. The mole-demons were a repulsive lot, but they were the most trustworthy beings in the Underworld. Hack would allow himself to be chopped to pieces before he would betray his master.

Arlo Cobalt. By all the gods, I am amazed your withered ass is still alive. Even your name disgusts me.

Roland's entire body cringed at the thought of Cobalt, the murderous White Witch Extremist who had dedicated his life to the extermination of those who practiced the dark ways. With his small but ferocious army, Cobalt had sought them out, done away with them in the most gruesome ways imaginable, and then left the remains for the Normal Ones to figure out. Roland had lived on the Earthly Plane then. He had met and fell in love with Adele Peabody, a White Witch. Since The Law forbade a Dark Witch and a White Witch to marry, Roland renounced his magical ways and lived as a Normal One so he could be with her. The two slipped away and went into hiding, hoping that in time, people would forget about their odd arrangement and find someone else to talk about.

For a while it worked.

Until Arlo Cobalt caught wind of it. It had been Cobalt himself who had tracked Tibbs down. It was his habit to save the most depraved of the Dark Ones for himself, and Tibbs had committed the unspeakable. Whether or not he had renounced the magical life, he was still by blood a Dark Witch. And now he had fathered a half-breed child.

Roland Tibbs had gone straight to the Underworld after his assassination and became Klaa, General of the Underworld. His beloved Adele had gone on to her next life with no pain. Deegie, his wonderfully strange half-breed daughter, had mercifully escaped, but Roland knew that as long as Arlo Cobalt drew breath, he would continue to search for her.

By the fifth day of her illness, Deegie had regained her ability to stay awake during the daylight hours, and she could get out of bed unassisted. It was also on the fifth day that she'd crept halfway down the stairs, seen the condition of her kitchen and living room, and absolutely insisted that the Altman brothers go back to their own place. She adored her friends and was truly grateful for their assistance, but even at midpoint on the staircase, the aroma of cast-off socks and fast food bags made her nose hairs curl.

Today she sat in the pink velvet chair next to her bedroom window, reading and watching the white snowflakes tumble from the sky and the soft brown horned larks flit though the branches of the pines. She'd felt well enough to shower today, and although it felt good to be clean, she didn't think she had the strength to do much else for a while. Her breathing had improved after the hot water, and as she drew in a breath, she smelled pine cleaner and furniture polish. The brothers must be taking care of the mess they'd made.

Zach had insisted on positioning a space heater in her window nook. Its warmth and constant hum, combined with its comforting orange glow, somehow reminded her of Tiger. Deegie clamped her eyes shut and fought tears. *No. Another time. I have enough snot problems; I don't need to be crying on top of it.* The fur-muffled thump of running cat feet, both ghostly and living, came from upstairs, followed by Lisbet's soaring soprano as she sang to Bast and the ghost cats. Deegie focused on that instead; it made her smile. She felt herself drifting off, but didn't fight it. *Gulliver's Travels* slid off her lap and thumped to the floor.

"Hey, Deeg?"

She opened her eyes and frowned. The Altman brothers stood in the doorway, looking awkward.

"Oh, hi." Deegie squinted. "When did I go to sleep?" She wrapped her afghan around her shoulders in a clumsy cape and stood up.

"Don't get up!" the brothers said in unison, then they turned and glared at each other, as they often did.

"I'll have to get up sooner or later. Especially since you guys are leaving." She motioned to them to follow her. "Besides, I want to survey the wreckage, so to speak."

Back down the stairs they all went, with Bast leading the way.

Deegie coughed into a tissue while she nodded her approval of the brothers' clean-up. "All right," she said at last. "I'll let you live. Thanks for cleaning." She winked and tilted her pale cheek in their direction. "Kiss bye-bye?"

"Deegie, I've wanted a kiss from you for months, but I wouldn't do it now for all the trout in Fiddlehead Creek. Flu-free, that's me." Zach opened the front door, and a blast of freezing air dashed in for a look around.

"Oh, brr. Jeez!" Deegie tightened her afghan cape and stepped backwards. "Be off with you, then! Be gone!" The brothers walked out into the freezing air, and she shut the door behind them.

"You're an idiot. Just thought you should know," Gilbert said to Zach as they waded through ankle-deep powder on the way to the Jeep.

"Huh? What's your issue *now*? Did I mispronounce something? Does my shirt clash with my socks?"

"You'll never get together with her, you know. You might as well stop trying, because she's clearly not interested. I can tell."

"What the hell is that supposed to mean?" Just as Zach turned to face his brother, something slammed into his side, and he toppled over into the snow at the side of the driveway.

After a quick check for broken bones, blood, and bruises, Zach sat up, unhurt. "What the hell was that?" he sputtered, wiping clumps of snow out of his beard. "Some kind of invisible sucker punch spell? You're a dick, Gil."

"No! I didn't do—" The rest of his sentence died in his throat and he stared hard at the snow-covered ground next to his fallen brother.

"What?" Zach swiveled his head and scanned the snow.

"Tracks," said Gilbert. "Look again."

Zach looked. A looping, weaving line of animal tracks cut across the yard. The tracks looked firm and clear, as if they had been made only minutes before. They resembled those of a large dog, a wolf perhaps, but even an amateur tracker could tell there was nothing normal about the creature that made them. The tracks suggested an animal with missing toes on one foot; something with a pigeon-toed, three-legged gait.

"Holy crap!" Zach traced a circle in the snow around one of the tracks with a fingertip. "What made that, genius? Huh?"

"I... I don't know," Gilbert admitted. "An injured dog, maybe?"

Zach got to his feet and brushed snow off of his jeans. "I don't feel right about this," he said. "Maybe we shouldn't leave Deeg here by herself. This thing might be dangerous."

"Well, it's not like she's going to go outside and play in the snow! She's sick, in case you've forgotten." Gilbert's voice held the haughty tone he affected whenever he thought he was right, which was often. "Now come on, I'm freezing my ass off."

The brothers argued all the way to the Jeep. They were still sniping at each other when they drove off.

In an unused room on the second floor, Lisbet peered through dusty lace curtains at the men in the yard below. She covered her mouth with her good hand to prevent the giggles from tumbling out, even though no one would hear them.

It was the first time she'd been out of the house in nearly a hundred years, and pushing Zach down was the most fun she'd had in almost as long. A smile of triumph creased her old face as she watched the men examine and exclaim over that nasty thing's footprints. They understood now, thanks to her.

'Twas real, she said to the ghost cat in her lap, 'twas real.

CHAPTER FOUR

Deegie re-opened The Silent Cat a full week after she'd hung the Closed Due to Illness sign on the front door. The place felt stale and clammy; the merchandise looked neglected and forlorn. Even after she'd flicked on the overhead lights and turned on the heater it felt as though she'd been away several months instead of a week. She let Bast out of his carrier and let him explore while the shop warmed up and she checked her messages. After a careful inspection of the colorful witchcraft shop, Bast waved his tail in an "all clear" and went to sleep on the counter next to a display of silver rings. The male kitten with the name of a goddess had left a trail of paw prints across the glass-topped counter, but Deegie didn't mind. The little guy had become a wonderful friend, and in her eyes he could do no wrong.

She glanced at the empty spot next to Bast, and the smile left her face. That's the last place she'd seen the antique talking board—and Tamara Biggs. *Shouldn't have left it on the counter,* she scolded herself. *Here's hoping she doesn't try to raise demons with the damn thing.* Deegie couldn't shake the feeling that she would be seeing Tamara again. Bad nickels always reappear.

Deegie set out a stack of newspapers for her customers and deliberately didn't look at them. She'd had more than her fill of the daily weird-creature-in-the-woods updates. The last she'd heard, the town's "experts" were now saying the mysterious being was definitely an alien from another galaxy. But still, people's pets continued to disappear, and that troubled her. She couldn't imagine losing Bast; the thought was too much to bear. Using the round table by the front window as a work station, Deegie set about crafting a basket of pet protection charms while she waited for her customers to arrive. She was certain they would sell well, and the scent of the dried cedar chips she stuffed the charms with soon filled the shop.

Her day progressed without difficulty, and she was touched by the number of customers who had missed her during her absence and were happy she'd recovered. Around lunch time, she received a call from a very excited Gilbert Altman. His flurry of words barged into her ear before she could even finish her standard shop greeting:

"Thank you for calling The Silent Cat, how can I—"

"Deegie, some hunters just killed a huge, deformed *something!* It just went down Main Street in the back of a pick-up truck! There are reporters from Anacortes, Pine Cone Junction—*everywhere!* You should see this damn thing!"

"Let me guess, they found it in the woods behind my house." Deegie was actually relieved to hear the news, but she couldn't resist the opportunity for a wisecrack.

"Uh, no, but at least you don't have to worry about that ugly brute wandering around in your yard anymore."

"I think that's the best news I've heard in a while. Maybe I can relax and enjoy my house now!"

"Yeah. Oh, *ugh!* That thing looked horrible! Gah! I wonder what sort of disease it had!"

"Yes, I saw it, remember? Oh well, I'm sure it will be on the news tonight. Thank you for letting me know, Gilbert."

The jingling of the bells tied to the shop's door handle announced another cluster of customers just as Deegie hung up the phone. In fearful tones, they passed the news of the dead creature between themselves:

"I heard that…"

"I saw it just now…"

"My cousin's the one who…"

"Someone said it was a…"

By one o'clock, The Silent Cat had become a gathering spot of sorts for Fiddlehead Creek's hardcore supernatural aficionados. Deegie had never heard so many different versions of the werewolf legend, and she had three more requests for silver bullets. By closing time, she'd sold every last one of the pet protection charms.

"A werewolf craze in Fiddlehead Creek. How 'bout that?" she chatted to Bast as she put him in his carrier for the trip back home. "Maybe I should capitalize on this and make werewolf protection charms next!"

Just as Deegie had predicted, the mysterious creature was the star of the evening news. At least a dozen photos, unedited and taken from different angles, flashed repeatedly across the screen, while the reporters took turns babbling excitedly about werewolves and chupacabras. While no one seemed to know *exactly* what the hideous thing was, it was certainly dead and the Fidos and Fluffys of Fiddlehead Creek were safe once more. Still, Deegie made a dozen werewolf protection charms while she watched. Even though the strange creature had been killed, werewolf fever was in full swing in Fiddlehead Creek; the charms would sell like proverbial hotcakes.

Any requests to visit the Earthly Plane had to be approved by the Council of the Underworld, and the erstwhile Roland Tibbs hated that. Despite the amount of time he had spent down here, he still loathed the fact that he had to ask permission to do anything. But his following this annoying rule was just for show; he was going above no matter what the Council's decision.

The Council usually consisted of six members, middle- to high-ranking business-demons, many of whom were successful—albeit corrupt—business *people* during their human lives. They wore identical black suits and dark sunglasses, which they never took off. Due to Roland's rank as general, this particular council meeting was presided over by none other than the Ruler of the Underworld himself.

The Ruler of the Underworld had many names: Satan, Lucifer, Beelzebub, Old Nick, Old Scratch—all of them invented by the living humans of the Earthly Plane. It was only the denizens of the world below who knew their ruler's *real* name: Steve. No last name, no middle name, just Steve. The humans of the Earthly Plane were always making up fancy names for things they didn't understand. Except for his serrated teeth and opalescent eyes, Steve looked very much like an ordinary human—a very tall, bald-headed one. He sat at the head of a long table made of bones, and he glowered at Roland when he entered the meeting chamber. Steve gave Roland permission to sit with a barely perceptible nod of his head.

Roland sat at the other end of the table, hoping the disrespect he felt wasn't showing on his face. The six council members were at the table as well, three to a side. The lenses of their dark glasses reflected the ever-present orange and blue flames of the Underworld. A spotlight snapped on above Roland's head, illuminating him in a dazzling cone of light. The council members squared their shoulders, their faces grim and impassive.

Steve rose from his chair. His bald head gleamed. "Klaa, General of the Underworld, formerly Roland Tibbs of the Earthly Plane, why do you seek permission to go above?"

Roland cringed inwardly; he hated his Underworld name. Klaa sounded like the noise a duck would make if someone stepped on its head. He wove his fingers together tightly and cleared his throat before pleading his case. "An assassin is stalking my daughter. I request permission to go above, find him, and kill him before he kills her. He is the same assassin who took my human life and that of my wife."

Steve's expression changed from bored to slightly interested. "You mean Arlo Cobalt? I'm surprised that old man's still alive." He quirked his lips in what passed for a smile and sauntered over to the other end of the table.

"And your darling daughter, Deegie Tibbs," Steve continued. "She's the one who opened an unauthorized portal to my kingdom and disabled one of my top gatekeepers, isn't that right?"

Roland nodded, keeping his eyes respectfully downcast.

"I thought so," Steve said. "We've been watching her, you know. We've left her alone—for now." His smile widened, revealing his serrated teeth. "It might be a good idea to let Cobalt follow through with his plan. Deegie would be a good candidate for the Underworld; don't tell me she wouldn't be. She seems to have a vast knowledge of things that are—shall we say—dark. Isn't that right, Klaa? If she were down here, you'd get to see her all the time, wouldn't you?"

"Cobalt is a good candidate. Deegie is not. She is clever, yes, but her heart is pure. It is my fault that she knows of the dark ways." Thinking quickly, Roland added, "Meaning no disrespect, sir."

Steve's laughter filled the council chamber and drilled into Roland's ears. "From what I know of Deegie Tibbs, I'd say she's more than capable of taking care of herself. Who knows, she might just kill Cobalt instead of him killing her!" The mirth dropped from his face, and his look of scorn returned. "Your request is denied, Klaa. You may return to your duties."

Steve turned away without further comment and headed for the chamber door, motioning the six council members to follow him.

Roland wasn't surprised; this was exactly the response he had expected. He buried his face in his hands in feigned despair, just in case Steve and his minions were still observing him through some secret peephole or scrying bowl. He held this pose for several seconds, and then exited through the still-open door.

He came up with the perfect solution the next afternoon. He got the idea from watching the Hell Hounds that roamed the Underworld. They were as diverse as the hounds of the Earthly Plane, and their sizes ranged from that of a tiny teacup Chihuahua to a massive Great Dane. It was a common sight to see the mole demons going about their duties with their adopted Hell Hounds in tow. Some even took their pets along on their excursions to the Underworld. Maybe it was time for Mr. Hack to get a new pet.

During his time as a Dark Witch on the Earthly Plane, Roland had perfected the art of shape-shifting. He still had these abilities, but, banished to the Underworld as he was, there had been no reason to use them until now. In the secluded corridor, Roland experimented with a new look after tending to Tiger Spirit. Seated on his usual boulder, he leaned forward with his head in his hands and thought of nothing but a gigantic hound with black fur and piercing blue eyes. In the pit of his brain, something tightened, flexed, and *popped*. There were no theatrical flashes of light, no billowing puffs of smoke, just a huge, shaggy canine occupying the space where Roland had sat just seconds before. Roland wagged his tail, yapped at Tiger Spirit, then returned to his usual form. Yes, this would work nicely. Chuckling to himself, Roland summoned his servant.

After hearing about his master's plan, Hack shuffled his feet and cleared his throat repeatedly. "Meaning no disrespect, sir, but are you sure this is safe?"

"Dear Mr. Hack," Roland replied, "You worry too much. Of *course* it's safe! No one will suspect a thing. Just another harried mole-demon out for a stroll with his pet Hell Hound, right?"

"But sir, if someone notices you're missing—"

Roland shrugged. "The Underworld is a big place," he said. "And even though I'm not allowed to leave it, I *am* a high-ranking official.

It would be a bit unseemly for anyone to question my whereabouts, don't you think?"

"Yes, I suppose it would, but…" Hack scratched at his crotch and made a troubled humming sound deep in his throat. "Yes sir," he finally said, "that is a brilliant plan. I would be honored to assist you."

"Excellent, Mr. Hack. That will be all for now. You are dismissed until I work out the finer details. Oh, and one more thing. I will be needing a collar and leash, just for effect, of course. Nothing pink, please."

By the next day, Roland and Hack had gone over their plan enough to put it into action. Hack, sweating in his human guise, stood in line at the main portal with the other mole-demons, waiting for his day pass to the Earthly Plane. Standing at his side at the end of a long vermillion leash was a majestic, solid black Hell Hound with crystal blue eyes.

"Where'd you find that one, Hack?" one of his colleagues wanted to know. "He's a beauty!" He extended his hand, as if to pat the hound's head, then pulled it back. "Does he bite?"

"Yes." Hack nodded. "He does, and quite viciously." He yanked hard on the leash in a show of authority. "Heel, boy!"

Roland, in his new Hell Hound form, growled a low, rumbling warning.

"Ain't that something!" The other mole-demon leisurely explored his nostrils with a grimy finger.

"Indeed it is," said Hack. The line moved up another notch, and he stepped forward with his hound.

"Here you are, Mr. Hack." A violet-haired service demon extended her claw through the booth window and handed him his pass. "Beautiful hound you have there. Enjoy your visit to the Earthly Plane, and come home soon!"

"Yes, yes, I will. Thank you." Hack tucked his pass into a pocket of his overcoat and stepped through the portal with his new Hell Hound.

For secrecy's sake, the Fiddlehead Creak portal opened in a secluded alley behind a strip mall on Bodem Street. The only witness to Hack and Roland's abrupt appearance was a homeless gent rifling through a dumpster. He gave them a cursory glance and returned to his task, but Roland waited until he stumbled away with his sack of cans before switching to human form.

"And here we are," Roland said calmly. "We made it through without a single mishap. Really, Hack, you need to stop worrying so much; it'll give you hypertension."

"Yes sir." Hack tugged on the collar of his shirt. "First order of business, sir?"

"Why, we find Deegie, of course!"

Roland had chosen to appear as a young blonde man for his trip to the Earthly Plane, since there was always a chance he'd be recognized. It felt sublime to be young again. And the sun! It had been so long. Far too long. He breathed in air scented with pine and mid-winter chill, gulping it greedily and wishing he could taste it as well. After breathing in the stench of sulphur and despair for so long, the aroma of Earthly Plane oxygen was ambrosial.

"Sir?" Hack squinted and blinked behind his round black sunglasses. "Everything all right?"

"Yes, fine." Roland ran a hand through his full head of hair and smiled with white, strong teeth. "Just enjoying being young again. Come along, Hack. Let's go find my daughter."

Secure in the knowledge that a misshapen horror no longer lurked in the woods, Deegie meandered through her backyard, thinking of spring and taking in the rejuvenating sunlight. Much of the yard still slumbered under a layer of snow, and Deegie was anxious for it to begin melting away so she could start preparations for the cat sanctuary. Beneath the icy blanket of white lay the tiny graves of generations of cats, the beloved companions of dear Lisbet. Deegie had plans for that part of the yard, too. Perhaps a low wall of river rock surrounding the graves, or maybe a wrought iron fence with an elaborate archway.

The bones of Lisbet herself were buried just to the right of the cat cemetery, next to a cracked and crumbling bird bath where her murderers had hastily interred her. Although Deegie had offered to move her remains to a more suitable location, the old woman's ghost had flatly refused. She wanted to remain there always, next to the bones of her beloved cats, the only true friends she'd known in life. Deegie found this both ironic and heartbreaking, but she would honor her friend's wishes.

"Do you suppose we'll get an early spring?" a man's voice asked.

The voice came from the left, and Deegie whirled around with a startled gasp. A young man in his mid-twenties stood at the edge of the yard, watching her intently with eyes the color of a light blue sky. She had heard no snow-crunching footsteps to herald his approach; it was as if he'd just dropped off a pine branch and landed in the backyard.

"Maybe." she replied warily. "It's my first winter here, so I don't know. And this is private property, by the way."

"My apologies," said the stranger. "I wasn't aware of that; I saw no signs."

But instead of taking Deegie's subtle hint and continuing on his way, he simply stood in place, smiling and gazing at her in a way that made her even more wary.

Great, she thought. *Now what the hell's going on? Never a dull moment at 14 Fox Lane, that's for sure.*

"It isn't marked," she told him, and she made her way through the snow over to where he stood. "But it's private property just the same. Who are you and what do you want?"

"My name is Klaa," he replied, and his weird smile never wavered. "And I'm just passing through. I live back there." He cocked a thumb at the vast woods behind them.

Klaa? she thought. *What kind of name is that? Dutch? Swedish?* Deegie's brows puckered in an uneasy frown. Something about this guy felt off.

"I've hiked in that forest quite a few times," she said, her voice icy with suspicion, "and I've never seen any houses or cabins. Just trees."

"Perhaps you didn't hike far enough then," the man replied, tossing a handful of straight blonde hair out of his eyes.

"Maybe…" There was something vaguely familiar about this young stranger who called himself Klaa. Something about the eyebrows, maybe. Or the strong, square jawline.

"I'm sorry to have bothered you," he said, with a barely perceptible bow, "I'll be on my way now. Do be careful in the woods. Odd things have been known to happen around here."

"So I've heard," Deegie said.

The young man turned and walked into the woods, and Deegie watched until he was swallowed up by the thick pine forest. His trail of footprints going into the woods was clearly delineated, but it was the only one; there was no trail leading out. As she looked at where he had stood, Deegie noticed something else. The edges of his footprints there had widened at the edges—were widening still—and tendrils of steam rose from the centers, like something red-hot had been there. As she stood and stared at the bizarre phenomenon, an errant breeze rustled through the pines, and with it came an acrid, burning smell, a smell she was all too familiar with. Faint but still noticeable, it wafted past her nose then disappeared.

She ran clumsily through the snow to the back door, slipping once and falling to her knees. Once inside, she raced through the house, locking every window and door. A canister of salt from the kitchen provided an added barrier when she poured a thick line of the stuff across the thresholds and windowsills. Salt would not deter a human intruder of course, but any foul being from the Underworld would be unable to cross over it.

I am not dreaming. I am not sleepwalking. My fever is gone. I know what I saw, and I know what I smelled. She stated this firmly to herself and was prepared to repeat it aloud to anyone who doubted her.

As a final measure of security, Deegie snatched up Bast, summoned white light, and enrobed the two of them in its protective mantle. The black kitten struggled in her arms and protested mightily with strident mews. Her own heartbeat still roared in her ears even as she commanded herself to take slow, even breaths and think rationally. It was the smell that had instilled the initial panic; there was no mistaking the fulsome reek of the Underworld.

Her next instinct was to call Zach, but she dismissed the idea after a moment's consideration. She knew he would come to her immediately, but being a Normal One, there was little he could do to help the situation. Wrapped in the protective bubble of white light, Deegie brought up Gilbert's number on her phone and tapped the call button.

CHAPTER FIVE

Arlo Cobalt tightened the belt of his ragged terrycloth robe and glared into his scrying bowl. The vision he'd seen in the inky black water showed the dead body of the black dog-creature he had conjured to seek out Deegie.

"My hunter. They've murdered my hunter," the old witch whispered. He shoved the bowl aside, splashing ink and water across the table and shattering the disturbing, infuriating vision. "I shall make more of them then, better ones. An entire army of them if need be."

A paroxysm of coughing shook his frail body; his face suffused with blood and turned a violent purple-red. When he could breathe again, Cobalt shuffled back to his bed and stared up at the ceiling. The faces of his followers hovered there; their faces faded in and out. Magical symbols floated there too: pentagrams, and hexagrams, and sigils, all in comic book colors, symbols of his unflagging faith.

He'd spared the Tibbs girl's life once, and all these years later he'd come to regret it. Cobalt had seen what she'd done in the inky water of his scrying bowl. He'd seen her dealings with demons, the opening of the hell portal, the dark spells she'd used. She'd taken after her father; he should never have let her live.

The ghosts of his followers gibbered and drifted across the ceiling, and his tired old eyes tracked their movements. Cobalt was the only one left, the last of the coalition dedicated to wiping out every last one of the Dark Witches.

Cobalt turned his attention to the scrying bowl, still sitting in an inky puddle on the table. He could have sworn he'd put it away. He got out of bed again, grunting with the effort. He would have to stow his belongings before the servants came in. They just wouldn't understand. Cobalt poured the ink and water down the toilet, dried the bowl, then put it and the bottle of ink back in the closet—top shelf, way in the back.

Back in his bed, Cobalt rested—eyes closed this time—and plotted his next move in the assassination of Deegie Tibbs. His followers resumed their hovering and whispered among themselves. Soon the servants would be in, bringing his food.

"An army this time," he mumbled as he drifted off to sleep. "An entire army."

Gilbert lay on his unmade bed, wearing just his boxer shorts and watching cartoons on a portable T.V. The three-bedroom house he shared with his brother was an absolute wreck, but screw it. He was warm, and comfortable, and more than a little drowsy. Besides, it was Zach's turn to clean the place up anyway.

The ringing of his phone interrupted his mindless viewing, and he had to search through his rumpled blankets to find it. He sat up straighter when he saw the number on the caller ID. Deegie almost *never* called him; usually it was Zach who got the phone calls. Wide awake now, Gilbert muted the TV and answered with a cheery hello.

"Gil? Is that you?" Deegie's voice sounded hectic and breathless.

"None other." He frowned. "You okay, Deeg?"

"I just… can you… can you come by right now? I need you."

Gilbert swung his legs over the side of the bed and stood up. "Of course. Is everything all right?"

"Yes. And no. I just really need you over here right now."

"Sure thing," Gilbert said, curious and puzzled at the same time. "I just need to hop in the shower first, and I'll be right there, okay?"

"Hurry. Please." Deegie hung up.

"It's about time you got your ass out of bed," Zach said when Gilbert stepped out of his room. "Who were you talking to in there, your inflatable love doll?"

"Very funny, but no." Gilbert sniffed. "I was talking to Deegie."

"Oh bullshit," Zach snorted.

"No, really. She said she needs me."

"You're kidding. Is she okay? She's not sick again, is she?"

"No, I don't think so. All she said was she needs me, and to please hurry." Gilbert saw his chance to tease the crap out of his brother and took advantage of it. "Why do you ask?" he added. "Are you jealous or something?"

"Hell no," Zach said. "She probably just wants to tell you in person what a douchebag you are. Seriously though, did she sound okay? Did it sound like an emergency?"

"Dude, relax. She probably just needs to discuss magic or spells with me or something like that."

"You're right," Zach said with a nod. "Why else would she be calling *you*?"

Half an hour later, Gilbert stood at Deegie's door with his hair still wet and his shirt untucked. When she let him in, the smile died on his lips when he saw the look on her face.

"Deeg? What happened?"

"Get in here, and I'll tell you," she said. She took his arm and steered him into the living room, then dropped to the couch and covered her face with her hands.

Gilbert saw she had lined the living room windows with salt, and alarm rose tingling into his chest. The only reason one would line doors and windows with salt was to keep out evil influences. He lowered himself to the couch and considered draping a comforting arm around her shoulders. "Well this can't be good," he said. "You want to tell me what's going on here?"

She surprised the hell out of him by sagging against his shoulder. "Gilbert, there was a man from the Underworld in my backyard this morning." she said.

"*What*? Deegie, that's just—"

"Ssh! Don't say anything yet. Just listen to me for once, will you? I need your help, Gil, not your lectures."

"Okay, okay. I'll try to keep my mouth shut. Just tell me, Deeg. I'll listen."

Although he was fully aware of the seriousness of the situation, Gilbert couldn't ignore the fact that he'd never been this close to Deegie before. Her hair smelled like incense and candles. When she'd finished telling her strange tale, she pulled away from him and sat up straight, as if she'd suddenly realized she'd been pressed against him.

"It was like I knew him somehow," she said. "There was something so familiar about him."

At Gilbert's insistence, he and Deegie went to the back of the house to look at the footprints left by the mysterious young man. They certainly *did* appear melted around the edges: elongated and widened to the point that they no longer looked like human footprints. A single trail of these prints—holes, really—led into the woods, just as Deegie had described.

"You say you smelled something too?" Gilbert hunkered down next to one of the prints, studying it, but not really sure what he was looking for.

"I smelled the Underworld," Deegie said. "Once you've smelled a stink like that, you never forget it."

"Yeah, that's for sure." Gilbert suppressed a shudder; he remembered that horrid smell all too clearly himself. He stood up and brushed the snow from his knees, his eyes still on the trail of prints. "I'd like to see where those footprints end. Go on back in the house. Seal everything, and keep white light around you at all times." He pulled a beanie out of his coat pocket and tugged it down low on his forehead. "I'll be back soon."

"Wait, you're serious? Are you nuts? You can't go alone!"

Gilbert considered this a moment as he studied the trees, then turned to Deegie and smirked. "Deeg, really. I'm perfectly capable of going for a walk through the woods."

"Damn it, Gilbert, don't be a smart-ass! You don't know what's up there! Just stay here. We'll figure out something else."

He cocked his head to one side and quirked a brow at her. "Hmm. Sounds like you might actually care about me after all," he said teasingly.

"Of course I care about you, dumb-ass!" she said with a roll of her eyes. "You're my friend! I just—don't go up there alone, okay? That guy was really creepy. Seriously."

"I'll be fine," he insisted. "If you recall, I'm one of the most experienced witches in the state of Washington."

Deegie glared at him, arms and legs akimbo. "I seem to recall having to save your ass from a certain demon not long ago. Don't tell me you forgot about *that*, Mr. Experience."

Gilbert coughed into his gloved hand and shuffled his feet on the snowy ground. "Yes, ah… let's not discuss that, shall we? It was a momentary lapse of reason on my part."

He refocused on the forest and the tracks leading into it. "I'm just going to go up a little way, just to check things out, okay? I'll be right back. Promise." He pretended to cringe at the angry look on Deegie's face, then took her gently by the shoulders. Before she could protest, he pressed a kiss onto her cheek. "There. Something to remember me by just in case I'm attacked by demons or carried away by flying monkeys."

"Yuck," Deegie said mildly, wiping the side of her face. "All right then, if you insist. Just be careful, okay?"

"I'm always careful," he said, and he turned and jogged off toward the forest.

The angle of the climb was steep and the footing was treacherous in the shin-deep snow. When the side of the hill leveled off into a flat spot, Gilbert stood in late morning sun, catching his breath and watching the smoke rise from the chimney of Deegie's house, far below. He was pleased with his speedy progress and congratulated himself on keeping up with his workouts; the climb was more intense than he'd first thought.

The trail of footprints continued on up the hill, weaving in and out through the trees, but it was the only unusual thing he'd seen so far. The air was scented with pine and the faint promise of spring; there wasn't the slightest trace of Underworld funk. Still, Gilbert believed Deegie's story, and he was more than a little curious about what might be lurking here in the thick of the woods.

Once his breath came easily again, Gilbert continued with his expedition. As he followed the trail ever upward, his thoughts returned to Deegie. What was with that girl, anyway? Talk about a bag of mixed signals! One minute she was pillowed against his shoulder, and the next, she was scowling at him and wiping his kiss off her cheek. It was as if he—and his brother, come to think of it— were permanently in the "friends only" category.

She sure is pretty, though, he thought, *and if she did something about that weird makeup and those horrid outfits, she'd be downright gorgeous.*

As he neared the top of the rise, Gilbert noticed something else: the forest was completely silent. Normally, on a sunny day like today, legions of winter birds chirped and squawked in the pine branches.

The cloudless sky was void of anything that flapped, fluttered, or soared across that endless field of blue. It was like something had frightened them all away.

The tracks ended near the top of the hill, coming to a halt directly in front of an outcropping of granite boulders. The largest one had cracked down the middle, giving it the appearance of a gigantic pair of buttocks. The tracks terminated there, leaving the strangest impression that whoever made them had walked directly into a huge ass made of stone. Under different circumstances, Gilbert would have found this absolutely hilarious.

The crack in the rock was about two feet wide, and the edges were scorched black, reminding Gilbert of the sooty mess on the back wall of a fireplace. When the breeze shifted, he wrinkled his nose as he caught the singular stench of the Underworld. Gilbert's heart rate spiked; it had nothing to do with his exertions this time. Fighting his instinct to turn and run back down the hill, he crept closer to the cracked boulder and peered into the dark crevice. Something shifted inside, followed by a sound somewhere between a cough and a growl. Two round lights, the color of jack-o-lantern flames, appeared in the darkness of the crevice. A second later, Gilbert realized they were eyes. Eyes that grew closer as the animal they belonged to rushed towards him.

Gilbert had no idea he could run so fast. His legs pistoned up and down as they carried him downhill through the snow. He heard no sounds of pursuit and wasn't entirely sure that the yellow-eyed thing even left the rock crevice, but still he kept going with the stench of the Underworld still in his nostrils.

CHAPTER SIX

"I saw her, Hack," Roland said for the third time. "I saw my daughter, and she's beautiful."

Hack, loyal and patient as always, nodded his head. "Yes sir. She certainly is. So happy you could see her again."

Hack didn't look happy about the close confines of their Earthly Plane hideout, however. It was dark and cramped, and Tiger Spirit took up most of the available room. Hack had not been required to don his human form this time, but he wouldn't be here long; he'd fulfilled his master's wishes for now.

The narrow crack in the rock opened up into a small, subterranean anteroom, and at the back of this hidden cave, Hack had installed a portal leading back to the Underworld. Now Roland could come and go as he pleased, and in any shape he chose. He checked over Tiger Spirit once more before returning to the Underworld. He would be fine here by himself now. The clean, fresh air of the Earthly Plane was better for him. Roland had grown fond of Deegie's guardian and was somewhat loath to leave him behind, but he would be returning soon enough.

"You're almost well enough to return to Deegie," he murmured to Tiger in an uncharacteristically gentle tone. "Won't that be wonderful? Just think how happy she will be. She is very near, just right down the hill, but you must not leave until I say. Understood?"

Tiger grunted and Roland felt a rough tongue rasp over his hand.

Although he knew that Cobalt's hunter had been eliminated, Roland could not rest easy until the old man himself was removed from the picture. Cobalt's conjuring powers may not have been as impressive as they used to be, but he was convinced that the old man was still capable of harming Deegie. There was always a chance that the next hunter he conjured would be successful.

Hack cleared his throat. "Ah... sir... not to interrupt, but we really should be going now. You are expected at the officers' meeting. They will no doubt be concerned if you are absent."

Roland nodded wordlessly and patted Tiger's head once more before slipping through the hidden entrance to the Underworld with his servant.

When Zach could stand it no longer, he took his phone from the pocket of his jeans and called Deegie's number. Gilbert had been gone for two hours now, and Zach still didn't know what was going on with Deegie. She usually called *him* when she needed help with something, and, as far as he knew, she really didn't care much for Gilbert. The mystery of it all was too much to bear.

Just calling to say hello, like I always do, he reminded himself. *Not jealous at all, nope, not me. Just calling to say howdy, and—*

She answered on the first ring, her voice strangely guarded and stiff.

"Deeg? How's it going?" He kept his tone light and friendly. *Just saying hello, that's all.*

"Zach. Hi."

"Is... uh... is everything okay? You sound, I don't know, a little off. Is Gilbert still there with you?" *Damn it, now why did you have to go and say that? It's none of your business if he's there or not. Deegie's not your girl, she's not* anyone's *girl, and she can do as she pleases with whoever*—

"Gil's not here, Zach. He's—he's following a trail of footprints up the hill for me."

"Wait—*what?* Since when is Gilbert an outdoorsy type? Come on, Deeg."

"No, really, Zach. He is." Zach heard a catch in her voice now, heard her draw in a huge, shuddering breath. "I called him because... because I need help again, Zach. Something happened, and I..."

"Deegie, you're not making sense. What's going on? Is *Gilbert* okay?"

"I—I don't know. He hasn't come back yet."

Just as Zach was about to announce that he was on his way over, he heard the distinctive slam of a door on Deegie's end of the line, followed by the sound of running footsteps and his brother yelling something unintelligible. That was enough; Zach hung up and grabbed his keys. He broke all posted speed limits on his way to 14 Fox Lane.

The feeling of déjà vu was strong in Deegie's living room. Here they were again, baffled by yet another instance of weird goings-on. Gilbert was none the worse for wear, despite his scare and his downhill sprint. Zach was still amazed that his somewhat metrosexual brother had volunteered to follow a trail of footprints up a steep and snowy hill, but he left it alone for now and listened to Gilbert as he repeated what had happened to him.

"It's the Underworld, alright," Gilbert said, nodding. He adjusted his chair so his snow-dampened pant legs were closer to the fire. "No doubt about it. Those rocks were as scorched as a barbeque pit. And that smell..."

Zach nodded ruefully. He too recalled the evil stench. "Maybe that Chul demon is out for some sort of twisted revenge. We did kick its ass, after all."

"The thought crossed my mind too, but if that were the case, then why didn't that guy just take care of Deegie right then and there? Why just walk off like that?"

Zach let out a long breath and laced his fingers together. "Yeah," he said, forced to admit his brother was right once more, "I didn't think about that part."

"Well *I* can't stop thinking about that thing in that little cave," Gilbert went on. "Another demon? Chul himself, maybe? Whatever it was, it sounded huge and pissed-off."

Deegie sat quietly with Bast as the brothers discussed this latest phenomenon. "I think he may have been one of my father's agents," she said when there was a break in the conversation. "I think he came to warn me."

"Your father had agents in the Underworld? And warn you? About what?" Gilbert leaned forward, his posture one of extreme interest.

"My father had strong connections to the Underworld, even after he renounced witchcraft, I'm willing to bet." Deegie stared into the fire as she spoke.

"Warn you about *what*, Deegie?" Gilbert asked again, an expression of alarm growing on his face. "Are you in danger?"

She nodded. "Yes. I've been in danger since my parents were killed when I was sixteen."

She told them then. The story of the events that took place all those years ago came spilling out of her mouth in a verbal flood that she seemed powerless to stop. She told them everything: the dinner party, the men who'd burst through the door, the screams, the dark sanctuary of the closet where she'd hidden for hours afterward, Moley, San Francisco. Everything. When Deegie finished her tragic tale, Zach was surprised to see that her cheeks were dry and her hands were still steady on her lap.

"Moley—I mean, Mr. Hack—never told me everything about my parents' murder, but he does tell me to be careful, to not discuss my past with anyone, and to always watch my back," she said. "He says there are people who would... would... hurt me if they knew who I was."

"You never told me any of *this*," Zach said, sliding closer to her on the couch.

"Well, it's not exactly good dinner conversation, Zach," she replied.

But her attempt at humor fell flat; he simply stared back at her, his eyes troubled.

Gilbert stood up, rubbed his hands together briskly, then sat back down. Zach had a feeling he was about to say something profound.

"Deegie," Gilbert said. "Your father was a Dark Witch, wasn't he? And your mother a White Witch?"

She nodded. "Yes. That's right."

Gilbert stood again and paced a circle once around the living room, tapping his chin and looking thoughtful. "Have you ever heard of Arlo Cobalt? Does that name ring a bell, Deeg?"

"No. It doesn't. Who is he?"

"You've been sheltered quite a bit, haven't you? Cobalt was what you might call a radical White Witch. He devoted his life to the complete annihilation of the Dark Flock. It was a huge thing right around the time your... well... around the time of your tragedy. You're *sure* you've never heard of him?"

"She said she hasn't!" Zach snapped, leveling his brother an irritated glare.

Gilbert kept talking. "A marriage between a Dark Witch and a White Witch would have infuriated him, especially if they'd had a half-breed child." He glanced at his brother and added, "Forgive me, Deeg. I know that sounds awful, but, well..."

"That's what I am," she said with a one-shouldered shrug. "Go on."

He cleared his throat and continued. "I'm willing to bet Cobalt had a hand in the murder of your parents, Deegie. I'm also willing to bet that you're right—that man came to warn you. Cobalt must have found out about the way you—we, I mean—opened a door to the Underworld. Strictly forbidden stuff for a White Witch, you know."

"He must have been stalking me for years, just waiting for me to screw up." Deegie slid a thumbnail between her teeth and began to chew. "All this time I've been convinced I was safe, that the assassin had moved on or died. No wonder Moley's always so full of warnings. He knows! He isn't just a paranoid delivery man, he knows Cobalt's been watching me all this time."

"Can't you just, I don't know, move away for a while, or something? Go somewhere safe?" Zach cut into the conversation. The thought of Deegie moving away to an unknown location was heartbreaking to him, but the thought of her being in danger was even worse.

"No," she replied with a firm shake of her head. "I don't run from anyone. Besides, what about Lisbet and The Silent Cat? And the cat sanctuary? I can't just abandon all that, Zach. I'll stand my ground."

"Sounds like we'll need an army of our own if we're going to take this guy on, then." Zach said morosely.

Gilbert took out his phone and scrolled briskly through the address book. "Alright then," he said. "Let's call in the troops."

"Wait, what are you doing? Who are you calling?" Deegie made a grab for Gilbert's phone, but he held it just out of her reach.

"You don't really think that you and I are the only natural-born witches in Fiddlehead Creek, do you?" Gilbert smiled mysteriously and winked. "I've got friends in high places. Low places, too."

By evening, Deegie's living room was full of witches, eight of them so far. They varied in age, gender, and affiliation—some White Witches, some Dark—but all of them shared a common goal: eliminating Arlo Cobalt once and for all. Nearly all of them had a story to tell regarding the murderous radical, and two of the Dark Witches present had lost family members to his violent crusade.

Deegie could not remember a time when she'd been in the company of so many of her kind. The feeling of camaraderie had helped to ease her fears, but still she had to keep wiping her sweat-slick palms on her skirt, and her smile felt too wide and strained. All eyes were on her, and she was beginning to feel like some weird sideshow attraction. In her nervousness she'd already forgotten half their names. She scanned their faces once more, trying to appear casual about it.

Okay, there's Danny Q., Nix, Jinx, and... and—oh dammit! Deegie hoped the others wouldn't notice her inner turmoil. This wasn't like having a busy day at the shop. Not even close.

"That would be just like Cobalt, spying on you like that, tracking your whereabouts. Yup, that's his style, all right." An enormous, bear-like man named Mike Rosenstraum spoke up. He rubbed his hands together and nodded, as if he was giving himself permission to tell the rest of the story. "That bastard took a girlfriend from me about ten years back," he went on. "Killed her dead as a doornail while she was collecting field mint down by the creek one day. Ain't never been another one like her." The huge man hung his head; his scraggly beard brushed against his broad chest.

"I'm sorry to hear that," Deegie offered cautiously. She felt uncomfortable when people spoke of deceased loved ones, especially when it was someone she had just met. Rosenstraum raised his head and smiled at her, much to her relief.

"Thank you," he said. "It was a long time ago, but I swear I can still see her face when I close my eyes at night." He blinked rapidly and nodded again. "She looked a little like you, as a matter of fact."

"I had a feeling Cobalt was up to his bullshit again when I heard about that creature roaming the woods over here." An older woman called Flower spoke up now. She moved closer to Rosenstraum and laid a hand on his shoulder. "Horrible man, that Cobalt, just horrible." She shook her head, making her long grey braids sway, and then reached over and patted Deegie's knee. "Sorry about your folks, sweetheart," she said.

Deegie nodded her thanks and fought tears. She liked Flower immediately; the woman had a calming, comforting presence that Deegie hadn't felt since she lost her mother. "I'd never heard of this Cobalt guy before," she admitted. "It's been a long time since I've been around other witches. I—I guess I've been a little sheltered. *More* than a little, actually."

"He killed my dad too," Danny Q. said quietly. "I don't remember it, though. I was just a baby. My mom talks about it every once in a while, though."

"I'm... I'm so sorry." Suddenly realizing that she was being a terrible hostess, Deegie excused herself, promising to return with refreshments for all. Once in the kitchen, she closed the door behind her and leaned over the sink, breathing deeply and hoping she wouldn't throw up. They were all here to help her, and she was both amazed and grateful, but things were just happening too fast. Life with her ex-boyfriend, Spencer, had been boring as hell, but it had been *safe*. The most stressful things she'd dealt with back then had been what to have for dinner, and whose turn it was to clean the dog crap off the carpet. Now her life was a non-stop thrill ride featuring demons and ghosts and the very gates of Hell itself.

Maybe it's the house, she reckoned as she splashed cold water over her closed eyes. *I've had nothing but trouble since I moved in. Maybe it's cursed or something.*

But of course that was ridiculous. This was just an old house with a weird past, and she was just a disabled half-breed witch who had been courting disaster for too long. But this time she wasn't alone, and despite her extreme nervousness, she was grateful for Gilbert and his friends. His *army*.

She dried her face on a dish towel and returned to the task at hand: preparing drinks and snacks for the cluster of witches in her living room. She heard the squeak of the kitchen door opening as she filled a bowl with tortilla chips, and she knew Zach was there without even turning around.

"Deeg?" he said. "Everything cool? Need any help, or... anything?"

She turned to look at him. His face was a mask of worry. She put the bag of chips down and went to his side. "I'm okay, Zach. Everything's fine." But she knew her tone wasn't convincing, just as she knew Zach hadn't really come in here to help her with the snacks.

"Everything's fine?" he echoed. "Hardly. It's far from fine, and you know it." He blinked at her, then took her in his arms. "Why didn't you tell me about all this? Someone's been stalking you all this time, and you never said a word. Why? I could have at least done... *something*."

She returned his hug, tightly, fiercely, then pulled away. "I appreciate that, but it wasn't any of your business, Zach. Not to be an asshole about it, but it wasn't." She softened the blow a bit more by giving him a peck on the cheek, then she pointed to the refrigerator and said, "There are some sodas and bottled water in there. You can help carry them out for me if you want."

She went back to the bowl of chips so she wouldn't see the pain in his eyes.

Once the snacks had been served, Gilbert stood and clapped his hands smartly for attention. "Okay everyone, listen up one sec, okay?" When all eyes were on him, he continued. "Just one thing you should know about Deegie here before we plan our attack. She has Witch's Cramp, so any huge energy expenditures will have to be up to us. Please respect that."

Now all eyes were on her once more, and there were mutters of sympathy. Deegie reddened and looked at the floor.

"Witch's Cramp? What the heck is that? Is it contagious?" Danny Q. spoke up.

"It's a disability that affects some Natural Born witches," Gilbert replied immediately (as Deegie knew he would). "She gets debilitating headaches if she tries to do more than a few spells at a time, and no, it's not contagious."

"Damn, that must suck!" Danny Q. said. "I've never heard of it before."

Deegie managed an embarrassed smile.

"I think we should begin by heading up the hill behind this house and checking out the little cave I found up there." Gilbert was taking charge once again and appeared to be fully in his element. "I'm sure there are enough of us here to take on anything that might—"

Something smashed into the living room window, hard enough to crack the glass. Deegie caught a glimpse of a black, hovering *thing*. It peered at her through the glass with glittering orange eyes. She scrambled backwards, away from the window. "What is *that*? Gilbert, what is that thing?"

CHAPTER SEVEN

Once the servants had finally left him in peace, Arlo Cobalt reclined in his bed and watched the faces of his followers as they drifted and bobbed across the ceiling. Strange how they chose to congregate there lately. Perhaps they would speak to him some more tonight before he began the second attempt at ending the life of Deegie Tibbs. They always had such wonderful ideas.

They really should have put more thought into the décor of this place, he thought as he watched his faithful flock hover and swirl above his head. The light fixtures were awful, the bedside chairs were dreadful, and that metallic circle right in the middle of the ceiling tiles looked out of place. What was that thing anyway, a speaker of some type, perhaps? But there was no music coming out of it; there was *never* any music, and that troubled him as well. He'd have to let the servants know about this. He was a very important man, after all. He tried to remember how long he'd owned this particular castle, but the information hovered just out of reach. No matter. He had more important things to contend with right now.

Ping! Perhaps a flock of birds, Mr. Colbalt. Mr. Cobalt, a flock of birds, please.

"An excellent idea, my faithful one," Cobalt replied with a toothless smile. He loved the way the tone sounded before one of the faithful spoke; however, he didn't remember instructing them to do so. Repeating their words was considerate as well. He had to admit he was getting a little hard of hearing. "A flock of birds it shall be. The most bloodthirsty birds the world has ever seen. Crows of death, yeah?" This struck Cobalt as extraordinarily hilarious, and he exhaled mad, wheezing laughter until tears leaked from his eyes.

A passing servant opened the door and stuck her head in. "Hush, Mr. Scott," she said, a finger against her lips. "Go to sleep now. You need your rest."

Cobalt glared at her. He could not remember her name, but she would be dismissed in the morning. The very nerve telling him to hush like that! And she couldn't even get his name right! Mr. Scott? Psssh. He was Arlo Cobalt, destroyer of the Dark Flock! Couldn't she see that? He had a brief flash of memory then, like a film clip from another time in his life. "Your name is David Scott now," someone kept saying over and over. Who was it? A woman's voice. "Mr. Scott... David Scott... say it with me... we can't let anyone know who you really are. They wouldn't understand. Scott... Mr. Scott..." The odd memory faded, crumpled in on itself, and disappeared.

Ping! Time is of the essence, Mr. Cobalt. Mr. Cobalt, time is of the essence.

"Indeed," was his whispered reply. "Indeed it is, my dear one."

He waited until he could no longer hear the sound of the intrusive servant's feet—she needed to be punished for something he couldn't quite recall—then slipped out of his bed and went to the closet where he kept his box of magical items. So many of them were missing, but they had to be around here somewhere. He got back into bed and spilled the contents of the wooden box onto his lap. Now then, a spell to summon a flock of winged assassins. He set up the necessary items in the proper fashion: a handful of black buttons, arranged in a circle; the mummified foot of a crow; a sprinkling of powdered dragon's blood. Cobalt frowned. Was that right? He uttered his wheezing laugh again. Of course it was right. He was Arlo Cobalt after all, and Arlo Cobalt made no mistakes.

With the image of a dozen huge, fierce crows in his head, Cobalt began his chant: "I call upon the power of the righteous... the righteous light..." *No, no, that's not quite right.* "... the power of the white... birds of vengeance will take flight..." *Wrong again, damnit. Have the servants drugged my food again? I'll fire them all!*

He got it right the third time. Close enough anyway. He'd forgotten the candles and an offering for the gods, but that was all right. Surely they would understand.

Ping! The spell is complete, Mr. Cobalt. Mr. Cobalt, the spell is complete, please.

"There, you see? It is done. Farewell, Deegie Tibbs." Cobalt nestled his head deeper into the pillow, and when he fell asleep he was still smiling.

Before anyone could fully react to Deegie's shout, something collided with the side of the house with a loud bang. Two more blows hit the roof. A window shattered on the second floor. Deegie heard the discordant tinkle of glass on tile coming from the upstairs bathroom, followed by muffled thumps and a strange rustling sound.

"It got in! My cat is up there!" Deegie leaped to her feet and headed for the stairs at a run, only to be restrained by Zach.

"Don't you dare go up there!" he scolded. "You don't know what—"

"Bast is up there! Let me go!" She wrenched her arm free and ran for the stairs.

Before she reached the first riser, Bast came hurtling down from the second floor, his paws barely touching the stairs as he ran. Pursuing him was a bird-like creature the size of a well-fed city pigeon. One side of its body was hideously oversized and skewed to the left. Despite its ragged, mismatched wings, it was somehow able to fly, albeit clumsily. Caught in its beak was a tuft of black fur.

In one swift movement, Deegie snatched up the terrified black kitten and raised her right arm in the direction of the bird-like thing. Her entire body clenched. The bright red bolt of fury that shot from her fingertips obliterated the lopsided flying creature and made a round, smoking hole in the wall behind it. A few greasy black feathers spiraled down to the carpet. A severed avian foot twitched and convulsed on the last step.

Another window shattered in the living room; cries of disgust and alarm followed. Deegie heard a thick, guttural croaking sound and the rustling flap of wings. She burst through the living room door with Bast under one arm, and the other raised defensively, ready to fire off another bolt if need be. A second bird creature was backed against the wall by the fireplace; Zach and Rosenstraum had it cornered. Zach brandished a fire poker, while Gilbert and the other witches looked on warily.

"What in the wide world of sports is *that* ungodly thing?" Rosenstraum's voice was oddly calm and even carried a hint of amusement, as if seeing hideously deformed birds was a normal thing for him. "Ain't never seen anything like that before in all my long years." He prodded at it with the toe of his boot. The hellish bird pecked at it and hissed like a snake.

This one was larger than the other. Its clawed toes—six on one foot, only three on the other—snagged in the carpet, and its three ragged wings beat frantically against the walls. When it opened its beak to squawk at them, the stink of long-dead road kill fouled the air. Its dull, dirty-orange eyes fixed on Deegie as she entered the room. It shrieked in fury when it saw her, its cries sounding like a very old man screaming out her name: *Deeee-geeeeawk! Deeee-geeeeawk!* Bast hissed in reply and struggled to free himself from Deegie's grasp.

"Kill that thing! Don't just stand there staring at it, kill it!" Flower elbowed her way through the cluster of witches. A concentrated blast of energy from the old woman's right hand reduced the bird-thing to a loose fluff of foul-smelling black feathers. She glanced at Deegie, standing there open-mouthed with Bast in her arms, and said, "I guess it's up to the girls to zap the evil beasties, huh? You okay, babe?"

Deegie nodded and pointed upwards. "On the roof. There are more of them. I can hear them."

Above their heads, clawed, malformed bird feet scraped and dug at the shingles. A series of soft thumps announced the arrival of more. Beaks scratched and pecked at the chimney bricks, and loud, furious shrieks echoed down the flue.

Flower took charge. Her caftan billowed around her as she turned and pointed out the men in the group. "You! Outside! Blast those cussed things! Cloak yourselves and watch each other's backs!"

Despite the dire situation, Gilbert still managed to look indignant as he followed the rest of the men outside. Zach went with them too, still clutching the fire poker. Deegie stood in the middle of the living room with Flower and a blonde woman named Nix. The three of them watched the windows, the broken one in particular, ready to blast anything that tried to come through.

On the other side of the glass, dark shapes flew back and forth through the gloom. She could hear their harsh, horrible sounds, and the purple twilight was pocked with the orange glow of their eyes. She knew she could only release a few more blasts of energy before the Witch's Cramp brought her to her knees, and she grabbed a pair of fireplace tongs from the hearth to use as a weapon. Better to save the rest of her powers for the most crucial moments.

A black feathered head thrust itself through the hole in the window, bringing its carrion stench with it. Its flaking, pointed beak snapped and pecked at the air as it tried to pull itself into the living room. Deegie raised the fire tongs, but Nix got there first and vaporized it with a powerful bolt from a wand she held in her fist. Feathers and stinking black gore splattered the window.

Deegie lowered the fire tongs. "Nice shot, Nix," she said, and she reminded herself to never again tease a witch for using a wand.

Something burst through the broken window upstairs; Deegie heard the rest of the glass fall into the tub. She offered Bast a quick apology, kissed the top of his head, then thrust him into the pantry and closed the door. He would be safe there for a while. The other women helped her shove the couch in front of the broken window and the three of them pounded up the stairs to fend off more of the feathered intruders.

A commotion on the landing brought them to a halt. A bird-creature was being torn to gory shreds by something diaphanous and gray. It swirled, dervish-like, around the remains of the intruder. Deegie saw gold and green eyes, so many of them. Pointed ears and long tails took shape and disappeared again. Lisbet's cats had joined the battle.

"What the hell is *that?*" Nix raised her wand again and prepared to fire.

"*Stop!*" Deegie grabbed Nix's wand arm. "They're ghost cats, they won't hurt you. I'll explain later. Let's find something to block that window with!"

Outside, the men circled the house, never losing sight of each other while they kept an eye out for the bird-things. A flashbulb-like blast of blue lit up the interior of the house as one of the women took out another flying horror. Zach held the fire poker like a baseball bat, ready to knock any approaching bird-thing out of the park. A dark cluster of them made a dry rustling sound, and their hooked talons ticked against the shingles. One of them sheared away from the hellish flock and circled through the purple gloom above. Falling like a stone, it dropped onto Zach's head.

"Shit!" Zach dropped the fire poker and grabbed for the ghastly thing. He ripped away a handful of black feathers. The bird-thing ripped and pecked at his scalp. Blood and sweat ran down his forehead. He swiped at the flapping nightmare again. Its hard beak gouged a hole in his wrist.

"Shit!" Zach screamed again. "Gilbert! Kill this damn thing!"

Something bright and hot flashed over his head. Gobs of sizzling bird guts slid down his neck, and the stench of burning feathers fouled the air. Gilbert's fire bolt had found its mark.

"I said kill it, not blow my head off!" Zach wiped clotted gore away from his mouth and eyes, and then puked extravagantly into the snow. When he raised his head, another avian monstrosity swooped out of the shadows. The foul beak clattered and snapped as it dove. He reached down and found the fire poker without looking, swung it, and connected. The mortally wounded bird plummeted into a snowbank in a shower of blood and feathers.

The rest of the birds flocked to the windows, fighting and tearing at each other in their haste to get at their intended victim. The ones on the first floor could not get past the couch blocking the broken window, and they hurled themselves against the walls of the house in frustration. The men were able to pick them off easily enough with short, lethal blasts of concentrated energy. Their bodies made hideous popping sounds, and the air was thick with the stink of burning feathers and hot blood. On the second floor, the bathroom window lit up with flash after flash of bluish-white light as the women took care of the intruders upstairs.

"I think that's all of them!" Rosenstraum's voice boomed from the side yard. "Zach! Where the hell are you?"

Zach lurched around the corner of the house with a hand pressed to his bleeding head. "Here," he said. He stumbled forward a few steps and fell to his knees in the snow. Rosenstraum went to his side, and Franklin, one of the younger witches, went to the other. Together they hauled him towards the front door.

"I can walk," Zach mumbled, trying to yank his arms free. "It's just a couple of scratches. I can walk!"

"Scratches, hell. You're bleeding like a stuck hog, Red." Rosenstraum lifted Zach off his feet and carried him over his shoulder the rest of the way.

Once they were in the foyer with the door closed and locked behind them, Rosenstraum did a quick head count: himself, Gilbert, Franklin, the guy who called himself Jinx, the twins, Todd and Kevin, Danny-Q, and Zach, the Normal One. All the men were accounted for and only one had been injured. Not bad for the first wave.

"That was a damn good shot with that fireplace poker, Ginger," the huge man said as he put Zach down in the hallway. "You play ball?"

"What...?" Zach squinted at him through the blood that kept dripping into his eyes. His knees were as wobbly as a palsied old man's. His bloody wrist was beginning to swell. "Was that thing poisonous or something?"

"Possibly." Although the question wasn't directed at him, Gilbert answered it immediately. "I did detect a strong odor of carrion on those things. But head wounds bleed like crazy, and that beak gave you a hell of a whack. Those two things alone would make anyone a little loopy." He took Zach's arm and steered him towards their makeshift living room headquarters. "Come on. I'll see if Deegie has a first aid kit."

Zach yanked his arm away and glowered at his brother. "I can walk, damnit!" He weaved his way to the living room, leaving a trail of red polka dots.

The women descended the stairs in a row: Deegie first, looking wild-eyed and fierce; Nix, scowling and clutching her wand; then Flower, sedately lifting the hem of her tie-dyed caftan and looking remarkably serene.

Deegie caught sight of Zach's gore-streaked face, and she quickened her step to a run. "Zach! What happened? Are you all right?"

Zach smiled crookedly through a sticky red mask. "A bird critter got me, Deeg. I kicked its ass, though." He turned his bloody head to include the rest of the women. "You girls okay?"

Nix tucked her wand into her purse with an unnecessary flourish. "Of course we are," she said. "That was a cake walk compared to some of the things I've dealt with." She peered at his blood-streaked face and frowned. "Maybe next time you should stay inside."

Flower also studied his face for a moment, as if assessing his injuries. "Young man, if you're not going to drop dead, I suggest you go and clean yourself up," she said. "You're getting blood all over Ms. Tibbs's clean floor."

"Come on, Zach, I'll help you with that. I have bandages and stuff in my bathroom." Deegie took Zach's arm and led him down the hall.

Once they were in the bathroom, Deegie closed the door and instructed Zach to sit on the counter while she rummaged in the medicine cabinet for gauze, tape, and antiseptic. "You shouldn't have gone out there," she said as she wiped his face with a wet washcloth. "Situations like this are even more dangerous for Normal Ones, you know." She wet a cotton ball with liquid from a small brown bottle and dabbed gingerly at the cut on his head.

"Yeah, I noticed that. I don't think the girls like me much, because—Ow! That *stings!* What is that stuff?"

"It's tea tree oil, an antiseptic. Hold still, and don't be a baby." She moved the cotton ball to the puncture wound on his wrist. "And I think I agree with Nix. Stay inside next time."

"Are you serious? Some asshole is stalking you and you want me to just stay out of it?" He took hold of her arm, interrupting her careful ministrations. "Not gonna happen, Deeg. I can protect you just as well as anyone else! You think I'm just gonna stand by and let you get hurt?"

"No, Zach. I just—I just don't want *you* to get hurt. Don't you get it? Everything I care about always seems to get taken away from me. Maybe I just don't want that to happen to you too, ever think of that?" She picked up a roll of gauze and began winding it around his head. "And I don't want to talk about it anymore. Now hold still."

Zach complied and was silent until she'd finished bandaging his wounds. "Look, Deegie," he said, "I know I don't fit in with the group. Hell, they look at me like I'm some sort of bug under a microscope. But I'm not going to just sit this one out, okay? I'm not. And I'm not going away unless you tell me to. Got it?"

Deegie didn't answer until she'd put away the first aid items. "Yeah," she finally said with a reluctant nod. "I got it."

CHAPTER EIGHT

Roland tried to relax against the cold stone wall of the narrow cave as he watched his breath billow out in white plumes and listened to the sound of Tiger's huge paws against the frozen ground. The mighty spirit animal was pacing again. He was almost as restless as Roland himself. Earlier that night, in his Hell Hound guise, Roland had stood in dappled moonlight at the top of the hill and watched the brief, fierce battle between the band of witches and Cobalt's flock of ghastly bird creatures. He'd been tensed and ready to jump into the fray, but it hadn't been necessary—not this time anyway. Deegie's friends had protected her well. He had no idea what sort of half-formed nightmare Cobalt might send out next, but for now, Deegie was safe.

He'd been tucked away in the little cave since then, meditating and ruminating. Despite the dismal circumstances, he enjoyed his time on the Earthly Plane, and although Hack was doing an exemplary job of covering for him, Roland reckoned he should slip back to the Underworld for a while. But first a quick lap around Deegie's house to make *sure* the area was secure for the night. Although he was impressed with Deegie's friends' abilities, they were still mere humans. And humans made so many mistakes.

Roland slipped out of the cave. The moonlight was nearly as cold as the air, and the snow made a delightful crunching sound under his boots. Halfway down the hill, he shapeshifted into his

Hell Hound form. His wide, thickly furred paws carried him over the snow with ease and he made it to the backyard of Deegie's house in a matter of minutes.

He lifted his nose and sampled the wind, testing it for any hint of human. The witches' cars still lined the cul-de-sac in a semicircle, but the windows of the house were dark and curtained. *They must all be sleeping in there,* Roland thought as he stepped further into the yard. There was blood in the snow, quite a bit of it. He hovered his nose over the frozen red splashes. One of them had been wounded; he detected human blood mixed in with the dark juices of Cobalt's bird-creatures. He moved closer to the house on silent, cautious paws, noting that someone had tacked sheets of cardboard over the broken windows. *That won't last long,* he thought. *Not against something that really wants to get in.*

A dark shape lay motionless in the snow a few feet from the house, and although Roland knew what it was, he went in for a closer look. To the casual observer, the dead creature looked like a large black crow with a bashed-in skull. Up close, however, all resemblance to a common bird ended. The thing had three eyes. One of them, open to a slit, showed a color like that of a dirty pumpkin. A single leg and foot, its talons clenched in death, protruded from the breast bone. This thing couldn't have roosted if it had wanted to. Hack was right about one thing: Cobalt couldn't conjure worth a damn anymore. His intention was stronger than ever though; Hack had been wrong about that part. Deegie was still very much in danger.

When Zach awoke, sometime around dawn, he couldn't decide which hurt worse—his head or his hand. He lay with his eyes closed and listened to the first tentative chirps of the forest birds while he decided. Deegie's couch was lumpy and uncomfortable. His arm was falling asleep. Finally abandoning the idea of a little more sleep, he sat up carefully, holding his injured head.

Jinx sat cross-legged on the floor, eating multicolored cereal out of a mixing bowl and watching cartoons with the sound turned off. Mike Rosenstraum lay sprawled on the recliner, his mouth hanging open and his feet dangling far off the footrest. Zach did not see any of the other witches, but he could hear his brother's lusty snore from somewhere down the hall. They were all still here; they had insisted. Deegie was one of their own, and they had treated her as such the minute they walked through the door.

"Hey, normal dude," Jinx greeted Zach amiably. "You're awake and you lived to fight another day! How's your head, bro?" He pointed to his bowl of cereal. "Want me to get you some munchies?"

Zach chuckled in spite of his discomfort. This guy was quite a character. "Hey," he replied. "I'll pass on that, but I'll take a pain pill if you've got one."

Jinx seemed to think this was enormously funny and he laughed merrily around a mouthful of cereal. "Naw, dude," he said. "No drugs here. The body is a temple, don't you know that?"

Have you noticed you're feeding your temple a bunch of sugar and preservatives? Zach thought. He remembered the pills Deegie took for Witch's Cramp. Maybe she'd give him one. "Have you seen Deegie around?" he asked.

"She's in the kitchen, I think." Jinx glanced around the room, as if he wanted to be sure they were alone, then added in a low voice, "Dude, Deegie's hot!"

"Yeah," Zach said. "Yeah, she is. Catch you later."

Deegie wasn't in the kitchen. Zach found her sitting halfway up the staircase, watching him calmly with Bast on her knees. He nearly walked right past her. If she'd heard the comments about her being hot, she gave no indication. She reached in the pocket of her skirt and took out her bottle of headache pills. She rattled it like a single maraca. "Need some?" she asked.

"Hell yes!" Zach took his grateful smile up the stairs and sat down beside her. He took two of her pills and dry-swallowed them while she watched him placidly. He could only imagine what must be going on behind those strange, beautiful eyes.

"I'll probably be taking some too before too long," she said at last. "I haven't slept. I couldn't stop wondering what Cobalt's going to send out next."

"We won't—*I* won't let anything hurt you, Deeg. You know that. How many times do I have to say it? We'll track this jerk down and end his career." He couldn't resist the opportunity to add something clever. "If you cut the head off a snake, it can't bite you anymore, right?"

Her smile was fleeting, and she lifted her brows as she looked at his bandaged head. "Very funny," she said. "And you look like the fife player in the Spirit of '76 painting." She stood up, clutching Bast close to her chest. "I'll be right back. We're going up the hill today, and I need to put some jeans on."

"Wait, are you serious?" Zach protested. "You can't go! You just got over the flu, and that's a steep climb!"

Standing in a shaft of early morning sunlight with the black kitten safe in her arms, Deegie sighed and rolled her eyes. "Zach, don't start, okay? I'm going. Period. I have this feeling that there's something up there I need to see. Something just for me."

"What? What sort of 'something'?"

"I dunno. I guess I'll find out when I get there." Deegie turned and climbed the rest of the stairs.

After a hasty breakfast, the witches assembled in the backyard. In the light of day the dead bird things looked even more gruesome than they had last night. Gilbert kicked snow over the nearest corpse before he addressed his army.

"I'm not *exactly* sure what I saw up there," he told the witches as he cocked a thumb toward the steep hill behind them. "Keep an eye out for a huge rock with a crack down the middle of it. It reeks of the Underworld, so you'll probably smell it before you see it. Like I said, I don't know what's in that cave, so be ready to blast it if needs be."

Nix took out her wand and polished it on the leg on her jeans. "My first dealings with the Underworld," she said to Deegie. "Don't worry, we've got your back."

The witches began their ascent.

Deegie fell behind immediately; her breathing was still a bit labored and phlegmy, but she refused to go back. She'd left Bast in the care of Lisbet, whom she'd finally located in the attic. The shy little ghost had hidden herself away after yesterday's events, and she'd become nearly frantic when Deegie had told her of her plans. "I'll be back," Deegie had promised over and over. But she'd left extra food and water for Bast, just in case.

Just as Gilbert had predicted, they smelled the cracked rock before they saw it. A ripple of unease ran through the group as their noses caught the acrid tang of the Underworld. Gilbert, at the head of the line, stopped and held up a hand to halt the rest of them.

"Smell that?" His voice was a low excited whisper, just loud enough for the others to hear. "We're getting close. Should be right past that break in the trees, there."

Deegie kept walking, continuing up the snowy slope until she stood at Gilbert's side. Diamonds of sweat gleamed on her forehead and her heart hammered wildly in her chest. She supposed she really *should* have stayed home, but she kept it to herself. She detected something else besides the smell in the air. It wasn't another smell, or a sound, or anything one could detect with the ordinary senses. This was something she felt with her gut, something she felt with her heart. It was near close enough to touch. It was something she lacked, something she *needed* without even knowing exactly what it was.

Deegie pushed past Gilbert and headed for the break in the trees. She found the double trail of footprints—the ones from the stranger, and the ones Gilbert had made yesterday. She followed them, head down and lungs burning. The split rock was near the top of the hill, in a wide clearing, and she stood at the edge of the trees, feeling the undeniable pull of whatever was inside. Vaguely, she heard the voices of Gilbert and the others yelling for her to slow down, to wait up. She tuned them out and listened to the blood whooshing and pounding in her ears instead. She stared at the rock, her gaze intense and unwavering.

The rest of the witches came out of the trees, sweating and out of breath. Deegie barely noticed them. She took a few more steps through the snow, extending her arms towards the crack in the rock and the mystery inside. In the darkness of the narrow opening, something growled.

"Deegie! Come back, damnit! You don't know what's in there!" That was Zach, but she ignored him too.

The voices of the others joined in, beseeching her to come back, to stay away.

The thing in the cave grunted, and two golden lambent circles appeared. Eyes.

Deegie stumbled forward, laughing.

"Deegie, stop!" Gilbert's voice rang out, iced with anxiety and sprinkled with fear.

Nix took out her wand and held it aloft. Gilbert followed suit, yelling, "Don't blast it yet! Wait 'til we see what it is! Deegie, come back!"

Something shot out of the cave. Unseen but still very much *there*, it moved across the snow in a rippling wave of motion, like a blast of super-heated air or a mirage on a desert road. It flowed over Deegie, engulfing her and pulling her to the ground. She laughed and laughed.

"Holy shit, it's got her! Blast it!" Gilbert fired a bolt from his wand, but it went wide. A sizzling hole opened in the snow.

Flashes of orange and black appeared in the diaphanous thing engulfing Deegie: stripes. The dark-haired witch rolled in the snow and laughed as though she'd gone mad. A bolt from Nix's wand sizzled overhead, and Deegie struggled to her feet to stand between the band of witches and the growling, flickering thing from the cave.

"Wait!" she screamed, spreading her arms wide. Tears poured down her face. Her joyful smile grew wider. "Please, stand down! It's Tiger Spirit! It's Tiger! He's alive!"

Gilbert spun around to face the witches. He raised his arms and shook his head wildly. "Wait! It's okay, it's okay. It's friendly; it won't hurt you!"

The witches stood in silence, awestruck as they observed the reunion between their newest member and her long-lost guardian. For just a moment, Tiger fully materialized, as if he wanted them to know just how magnificent he was. He stared back at them, uttering his feral grunt/growl. Then he wrapped enormous paws around Deegie and rolled with her in the snow. She laughed like a child, repeating over and over, "It's Tiger, it's Tiger! He's here!"

It was Danny Q. who finally broke the stunned silence. "Uh, can someone explain to me exactly what that thing is?"

"It's a guardian spirit," Flower replied before Gilbert could. She glanced at him briefly before continuing. "They are conjured on the eve of a witch child's birth. They are not pets; they come and go as they please. They stay with the witch child throughout their entire lives, protecting them from harm and offering comfort in hard times. It's an old tradition, dating back centuries. Not many witches do this anymore." She smiled at the sight of Deegie frolicking in the snow with the gigantic beast. "Beautiful creature, isn't it?"

Danny Q. swallowed hard and nodded. "I wish I had one," he said.

An unusual-looking man appeared at the cave's entrance, and Zach interrupted their conversation. "Deegie!" he yelled. "Look out! Behind you!"

Deegie spun around, still holding tightly to Tiger's neck. The blonde man who called himself Klaa stepped out of the cave; she recognized him immediately. He stood with his hands on his hips, watching her. A vague smile tugged at the corners of his mouth. Steam rose up around his feet as the snow he stood in melted and evaporated .

"I see you've found your Tiger," he said. "I suppose he's well enough to rejoin you now, Deegie. It was touch and go there for a while."

Deegie pressed close to Tiger Spirit and stared back at the blonde man, her eyes full of mistrust. "Who are you?" she demanded to know. "Why have you been keeping my Tiger from me?"

"Why? He was nearly killed in the battle with Chul, as I'm sure you recall, since it was you who opened the portal. His injuries were extensive, as were Chul's. What was I to do, let him die?"

Still kneeling in the snow, Deegie clung to Tiger and glared at the stranger. "How did you know that? Who the hell are you?"

"Hell indeed," the man sighed, and his eyes were full of sorrow. Tears overflowed and evaporated on his cheeks. Tendrils of steam rose from his face.

At the edge of the trees, the witches shifted nervously and murmured amongst themselves, ready to protect their own at a second's notice.

"Who am I?" the blonde stranger continued. "I am someone who cares. Someone who loves you very much."

"I don't know you." Deegie's voice came out in a strangled squeak, and she buried her face in Tiger's fur.

"But you do. Deegie, look at me. Look at me!"

She looked.

The stranger's features blurred and ran together. Piece by piece, his body became as dried husks that sheared away and vanished on the wind like laundry blown from a clothesline. His true form was revealed underneath. "Look at me and tell me you don't know me," he said.

Deegie stared up into the ice-blue eyes of her father.

CHAPTER NINE

Arlo Cobalt scowled at the black water in the scrying bowl. It showed him how he'd failed once more, and rage crept into his chest by slow degrees. That damn Tibbs girl! Damn her and all her damned friends! His beautiful flock of assassin birds had been annihilated, but how? How could they have done this? The spell had worked perfectly, hadn't it?

Ping! No spell is foolproof, Mr. Cobalt. Mr. Cobalt, no spell is foolproof, please.

"You shut the hell up! My spells *are* foolproof! They are!" Cobalt swiped his arm across the bedside table, splattering a mixture of ink and water across the blankets. The scrying bowl smashed on the floor. How *dare* his followers disrespect him like that! "Damn you! I'll kill all of you!"

His faithful flock remained silent. They hovered next to the ceiling, watching him.

His racket brought the servants on the run. At least *they* were respectful. He glowered at them as they filed into his room. One of them looked far too young to be an efficient servant. Her arms were full of—Cobalt squinted—infant supplies? Most likely for that brat in the other bedroom who screamed all night. And where exactly had that kid come from, anyway? He did not remember giving his servants permission to bring their illegitimate offspring into his home. "Get out of here!" he yelled at the young servant. "Leave my home immediately and take your mewling brat with you!"

The young woman jumped at the sound of his voice, dropping half the supplies she was carrying. "Mr. Scott, there's no need to—"

"My name is not Scott! I am Cobalt! Arlo goddamn Cobalt! Can't you see that?"

The youngster flinched and looked to the older servant for help.

"It's okay, Darla," the older one said. "Mr. Scott's just having a bad spell. It happens. I can handle this. You can go. They need that stuff in pediatrics."

Darla nodded and stooped to pick up her fallen infant supplies. She almost dropped them again in her haste to get out the door.

The older servant sighed, shaking her head at the mess on the floor. She knelt and began picking up the broken pieces of the bowl. "I'm not even going to ask what the black stuff is," she said. "Really, Mr. Scott, you're going to hurt yourself one of these days. We'll have to take everything away from you. Is that what you want?"

Cobalt reclined against the pillows and pretended to be asleep.

"I'll have to call housekeeping, I suppose." She straightened and took the broken pottery to the wastebasket in the corner. "And I know you're awake. Don't try to get out of that bed. I'm not above restraining you, you know."

You couldn't do that if you tried. Cobalt frowned. Had he said that out loud? And who was he talking to now?

The intercom pinged. *Nancy Rivas to Pediatrics. Nancy Rivas to Pediatrics, please.*

When he opened his eyes again, he was alone. The room was quiet and clean. Had he been sleeping? He lifted his head from the pillow and cast a scowl all around his bedroom. They hadn't cleaned very well. A small white box, only a couple inches long, lay half-hidden under the lowboy. He didn't have to look to know that the hidden end was covered with dust. They never did a proper dusting, and just yesterday he'd found an empty paper cup on the counter next to his bathroom sink. A *paper* cup. Revolting. Unacceptable.

Cobalt swung his legs over the edge of the mattress and stood up. After getting his bearings and finding his cane, he shuffled over to where the white box lay on the floor. He swatted at it with the end of his cane. Something rattled inside. He managed to bend over far enough to hook it with his fingers, and he took it back to bed with him to examine it more closely. It was a bottle of pills; he could tell by the distinctive rattle when he shook it.

"Drug addicts! Not only are they incompetent, they're drug addicts as well!" Cobalt said it quietly, but his voice was fierce.

He opened the box, and a second later he was laughing at his own folly. They were pills, all right, but hardly anything one could get addicted to. What he held in his hand was a bottle of homeopathic teething tablets for infants. The feeble-minded servant with the armload of disposable diapers and butt wipes must have dropped them. Idly, and for the lack of better things to do, he turned the box over and read the label. One word stood out more clearly than the rest: Belladonna. Really? In a medicine for infants? Incredible. It wasn't much; the whole bottle contained a miniscule amount, but still, belladonna was one of the baleful herbs. It was used in sorcery, and… and *war magic!*

Ping! It's time for war magic, Mr. Cobalt. Mr. Cobalt, it's time for war magic, please.

"Yes!" His whisper of glee was hoarse and sibilant. No wonder the other spells had failed; he hadn't used the proper ingredients! He slipped the bottle of teething tablets into the pocket of his robe and got out of bed again. His legs wobbled, threatening to give up and send him crashing to the floor. He held tightly to the bed railing until the feeling passed. Cobalt shuffled to the cabinet where he kept his meager belongings—it wasn't locked, despite the threats of the older servant—and took out his wooden box of magical supplies.

79

There wasn't a whole lot to work with; he would have to use substitutes again, but he had belladonna now. A tiny bit was all he really needed. War magic! Why didn't he think of this before? His palsied hands hindered the dig through the magic box somewhat, but he was able to find a few more key ingredients. He spread them out on the bed, keeping a close eye on the door. The vast hallways of his home were quiet now, but those servants couldn't be trusted. It would be just like one of them to interrupt the most important spell of his entire life: the spell that would end the life of the abomination named Deegie Tibbs. He supposed what he was about to do would be considered dark magic, but when it came to ridding the world of bottom-feeding scum like the Dark Ones and their unholy offspring, sometimes one had to break a few rules.

Cobalt cleared his mind and lit the stub end of a candle. There wasn't much left, but it would do. When the magical objects were arranged just so, he began his chant. The words…what were they again? He supposed he would have to use some substitutions there too, but no matter. This time it would take; this time it would work. In his mind's eye, he saw his new army rise up out of the winter soil, saw them lurch, and tear, and grab, and kill. They would surround the Tibbs girl and her miserable band of cohorts and reduce them to nothing more than a few red splashes in the snow.

Ping! The spell is complete, Mr. Cobalt. Mr. Cobalt, the spell is complete, please.

———✦———

"Dad? Daddy?"

Deegie stared up at the man in front of her. She shielded her eyes with her hand, thinking this was a trick of the light, a reflection of sun on snow perhaps. This man couldn't possibly be her father.

Roland Tibbs had been dead since she was sixteen. This must be a prank, some sort of cruel joke.

"Yes, Bunny. It's me. Come now, off your knees. Stand up. You needn't kneel before me."

It *was* him! No one else had ever called her Bunny. It was a term of endearment used only by her father. She staggered to her feet, using Tiger Spirit for support, and stood facing the only man she'd ever truly loved. Tears made warm streaks on her face. "Daddy. It's really you. You're not dead. But how? *How?*" She reached out to touch him.

Roland stepped back and shook his head. "You cannot touch me while I am in this body," he said. "I'm sorry, Deegie. And yes, I *am* dead. The human part of me, anyway. I am now a denizen of the Underworld. Do you understand?"

Although she didn't understand, not at all, Deegie covered her face with her hands and nodded. "I'm in trouble, aren't I, Daddy? He's after me now, because of what I did, isn't he?"

"Yes, Bunny. He is. And not just you." Roland lifted his chin to indicate the witches who were standing awestruck at the edge of the woods. "You've gotten them involved too."

"I know," she said bitterly. "I don't know what to do. Tell me what to do, Daddy. Help me."

"That's why I'm here—to help. An agent of mine has been looking into Cobalt's whereabouts, and we will be formulating a battle plan. We know he's near. Don't worry, Deegie. We'll fight back—together!"

Roland turned to face the cave and made a beckoning gesture. "Hack! I know you're in there. Come out; you won't be harmed. What more have you learned about our friend Cobalt?"

Deegie gaped at the pink, scuttling, naked thing that sidled out from the crack in the rock. She could her the gasps and exclamations of the other witches, and she laughed a little through the glaze of years on her face. "*Moley? Is that you?*"

The mole-demon, devoid of his human disguise, cast her a haughty look and sniffed indignantly. "It's *Mr. Hack*," he said. "I'll thank you to remember that next time."

Roland's lips flickered briefly in what might have passed for a smile, and he tipped Deegie a barely perceptible wink.

Hack cleared his throat and tapped a hind foot, as if he were waiting until he was sure the moment of brevity was over. "I have not yet located his hideout," he finally said, "but his last known residence was in Pinecone Junction, only a few miles from where we are now." Hack's hand wandered down to his crotch and he gave it an unabashed scratching. "Using a scrying mirror, I was able to determine that he spends much of his time in bed, but I am unable to pinpoint his exact location."

He paused to examine what he had caught under his fingernails, then continued. "The spells he's been using are weak; I don't think his... his... *conjurings* traveled any great distance to get here." He glanced at Deegie and Roland, then stared at the snow between his feet. "My own conjecturing of course," he added humbly. "Ah, sir, if you'll not be needing me, I'd like to return to the Underworld. I feel dreadfully exposed here."

"Mr. Hack, there is a chance I will be gone for a while so you'll need to make some excuses for me." Roland said.

"But sir, I... you..."

"You are *dismissed*, Hack!"

"Yes sir. Certainly sir." The naked pink mole-demon scurried away and disappeared back into the cave.

Roland smiled down at his confused, bewildered daughter. "Looks like you and I will be taking a little trip to Pinecone Junction," he said. "Just you and me on a little road-trip, just like old times."

Deegie's face fell, and her mouth dropped open. "What do you mean, road trip? Dad, there's no way I could possibly—"

"Hush," said Roland, his finger to his lips. "I will explain later."

Before Deegie could say anything more, he looked towards the group of witches standing in the trees and hailed them with a wave of his arm. "Witches!" he called out. "Come, let me meet you all! I am known as Klaa, General of the Underworld, formerly Roland Tibbs of the Earthly Plane, and the father of Deegie Tibbs!"

They came forward, hesitantly at first. Deegie coaxed them further, saying, "It's okay, you guys. He's my dad—sort of—and he's going to help us."

They introduced themselves, one at a time, until it was only Zach who hadn't responded.

Roland studied him for a moment, not unkindly, and finally said, "You're a Normal One, aren't you, young man?"

Zach blushed redder than his hair. "Ah, yes, sir. I am. I'm Gilbert's brother and Deegie's my... she's my friend."

"Your *friend*, eh?" Roland lifted his face to the sky and roared laughter. The sound of his sudden mirth dissolved the pall of apprehension hanging over the group, and a look of relief passed over the faces of the witches.

Deegie said, "Daddy, stop. Don't tease. Zach's a good guy." She lightly touched the bandage on his head and added, "And he's a good fighter."

Roland's eyes cut to the forest at the edge of the clearing. The mirth left his face; his smile disappeared. "We'll have to get to know each other another time," he said. His calm, flat voice belied his alarmed expression. "We seem to have company. Looks like Arlo Cobalt got a spell right for a change."

Deegie, Zach, and the rest of the witches turned as a group. Several humanoid figures stepped out of the trees. The breeze picked up, carrying a pocket of stench across the clearing: the nose-burning reek of decaying flesh. The figures began moving forward in a bizarre, shuffling march. As they drew nearer, it became clear that they had been dead for quite some time; some were little more than skeletons.

Rosenstraum spoke up first, his voice muffled by the hand he'd brought to his nose to block out the stench. "Zombies? You gotta be kidding me."

"Daddy? What are those things?" Deegie watched as the animated corpses struggled through the snow to reach them. "What's going on?"

"It looks to me like Cobalt's managed to resurrect a few of his dead followers," Roland replied. He shaded his eyes with the flat of his hand and squinted at the slowly advancing revenants. "Maybe more than a few."

More of Cobalt's dead followers emerged from the forest. They were in varying states of putrefaction. The meatier ones uttered low, guttural sounds as they lurched across the clearing. One lost an arm. Another's head fell off with an audible crunch; the body continued its inexorable march through the snow.

Tiger leaped to his feet and roared a challenge at the decomposing enemies. He advanced a few paces, ready to destroy anything that got too close to his mistress.

Although his face had paled considerably at the sight of this latest threat, Danny Q.'s voice was steady when he said, "They look slow and stupid. This shouldn't be too hard."

"Don't be too sure, young man." Flower pointed in the direction of the cave and the trees behind it. "Look!"

CHAPTER TEN

Faces appeared over the top of the rock. Some still had bits of flesh clinging to them; others were stark bone in various shades of white. Naked jawbones bared yellowed teeth in humorless smiles. A nimbus of stink descended on the witches, and it grew more nauseating with every passing second. Five more zombies crawled over the rock. Two of them lost heads and limbs, but managed to keep moving toward their intended victim.

Deegie raised her hands, ready to fire off one of the few blasts of energy she could muster. She knew the others would cover her once the Witch's Cramp finally rendered her powerless, but it was always painful nonetheless.

"What are you waiting for?" Nix lifted her wand and obliterated the nearest crawling horror. The zombie had been a juicy one. Gobbets of putrid flesh scattered across the snow in a starburst pattern.

The other witches followed suit; bolts of all colors and sizes hit their marks. Deegie heard Rosenstraum's hearty whoop of victory as he blasted two at once. Something whiffled through the air a scant inch from her head, stirring her hair as it passed. Thick, greenish slime splashed her face. An eyeball with a hazy pupil landed in the snow in front of her. She wrenched her face away, scrubbing wildly at the goo on her cheek with her cold fingers.

Tiger hovered over her. His angry roars thundered up and down the hillside. Deegie drew strength from that sound. She knew that as long as Tiger was by her side these walking meat puppets couldn't touch her, but still she felt obligated to do her part.

Five of Cobalt's resurrected followers emerged from the forest in a shambling cluster, and Deegie focused on them. She raised both hands in their direction. Something in her brain slipped up a notch, and she braced herself for the coming blast. Red fire spewed from her fingertips. Sparks sheared off from the enormous bolt of energy like a shower of tiny rubies. The group of zombies exploded into a stinking brown mist.

Deegie fell back. One of the witches—she didn't know which one—sent a bolt rocketing over her head. Glittering blue sparks trailed behind it. She heard the meaty *crack-splat* as it hit its target a few feet away. A stench like frying road-kill filled her nose.

How many are there? The thought roared in her head as her brain scrambled to reset itself. *How many followers did this guy have?*

Tiger stood over her prone body while she recovered, and she could feel his fur brushing against her face. She was thinking clearly, and although her head and body hummed and tingled, there was no pain. The Witch's Cramp hadn't taken hold yet; she would be able to fire again.

"Tiger, let me up!" Deegie shoved at her guardian's belly, trying to move him aside. "I'm still okay, I can do one more! Let me up!"

Tiger suddenly shifted to the right, and when Deegie slid out from under him, she saw the reason why. He reared up on his hind legs, briefly showing himself in flashes of black and orange. An image of his massive paw appeared, claws extended, and it flickered like a strobe light as Tiger knocked a flying zombie out of the sky.

They fly? These damn things can fly? Deegie sat up as another one dive-bombed Tiger. She caught a brief flash of a disintegrating, eviscerated corpse wearing a pair of gigantic black wings. Tiger reduced it to ribbons of decayed flesh with another swipe of his strobe-light paw.

Another one swooped in from the other side, and Deegie interrupted its dive with a quick burst of red light. Her already limited power supply dipped even lower—her scalp tightened; the Witch's Cramp loomed. The head of the thing she blasted hit the snow and rolled to a stop against her foot. An oversized bird's beak jutted out where its nose should have been. A single eye rolled over and fixed her with a baleful stare. The beak opened and snapped shut, and the creature went motionless.

Zach appeared at her side, holding a thick piece of tree branch in each hand. "Don't do any more!" he yelled. "You're going to hurt yourself!"

A winged zombie dropped low in the sky behind Zach, heading directly toward him. Deegie fired a final bolt over his shoulder that depleted the last of her energies. It caught the flying corpse broadside, and it plummeted toward the ground with a streamer of jellied guts trailing behind it. It smashed into the side of the split rock with a sound like a bag of pudding hitting a brick wall.

Deegie clutched at her head with both hands and dropped to the snow. The Witch's Cramp tightened around her, and the sound of her own blood pounding in her ears drowned out the noise of the battle. She felt herself being dragged; hot, steamy breath blew against the back of her neck.

Tiger, she thought, *dragging me away. Has to be him.* She forced her eyelids open to half-mast and saw huge black paws on either side of her head. She swiped blindly behind her head with both hands and her fingers touched long, dense fur. Not Tiger.

She tried to scream out for Tiger, for Zach, or Gilbert, *anyone*, but the pain in her head was monstrous. She could only manage a weak, high-pitched whine as she was dragged through the mouth of the cave. She aimed another feeble swat at whatever was dragging her, and her father's voice spoke, close to her ear.

"You'll be okay in here. Your Tiger will guard the entrance."

"What? Daddy...?" Deegie opened her eyes again. A gigantic black dog stared back at her. She sat up with a mighty effort and pushed the hair out of her eyes. Her vision greyed out and faded. "Dad! *Help me!*"

"Lie down!" he commanded. "I'll explain later."

Her eyes refocused just as the dog slipped through the crack in the rock and back out into the fray. Deegie heard distinct canine snarls and the sound of snapping bone. Through the narrow cave entrance, she saw a zombie with jerky-like flesh hanging from its rib cage. It fell backward into the snow, minus its head and one arm. She sensed Tiger somewhere nearby, grunting and pacing, and she willed herself to relax; Tiger would not let anything happen to her.

She sank back down to the dry floor of the cave, the motion sending a fresh lance of pain shooting into her overworked head. *Where did the dog come from? Am I hallucinating?* She focused on her breathing—that usually helped a little—and curled into a tight ball on the pebbled ground. She massaged her temples vigorously, imagining the scent of lavender, the sound of distant birdsong, and the feeling of warm, healing white light. But the noise from outside was too loud, too harsh; she couldn't focus. *Haven't they gotten them all yet?*

A singular sound cut through the din: high, and piercing and awful: the sound of a man screaming. Deegie clapped her hands over her ears. *Please don't let it be Zach! Please don't let it be Gilbert!* The scream rose higher, spiraling upwards like a siren until it was silenced by a wet, ripping sound.

———◆———

Arlo Cobalt was feeling good. He'd had to use one of those abominable paper cups for scrying since he'd broken his bowl, but it held the ink and water mixture just fine. Cobalt peered into the black water. His lips moved in a barely audible whisper. "Magic window, scry for me. Show me what I need to see."

A mist formed over the surface of the water. It rippled, swirled itself into a half-dozen fantastic shapes, then cleared away to reveal a vision for Cobalt. He saw Deegie, lying motionless on the ground. Her face had gone as white as the snow, and her eyes were closed to mere slits. Was she dead? Was he victorious at last? The vision segued into another scene, one of a flat spot on a snowy hill where his resurrected followers were engaged in battle with the Tibbs woman's friends. They were doing well, those followers of his. He hadn't planned on combining spells, however. Many of his intrepid faithful sported wings and beaks—how had that happened? No matter. It was working wonderfully.

"Delightful!" Cobalt cackled. "Just delightful! Kill them *all*, my faithful flock! Kill *all* of them!"

A hand appeared over his shoulder and snatched away his makeshift scrying bowl. Inky water splashed over the front of his robe. He looked up to see his head servant, and he scowled at her from beneath bushy brows.

"I think that's it, Mr. Scott. You've had enough warnings."

The servant yanked a handful of paper towels from the dispenser by the sink and dropped them on his lap. "Here," she said brusquely, "Clean yourself up. And where do you keep getting that black stuff?"

Cobalt said nothing. A grin still hovered around his lips. After the triumphant vision he'd seen, he couldn't help himself. He watched silently as the servant picked up his ink bottle and his wooden box of magical items.

"You're either going to hurt yourself or someone else, Mr. Scott. All this… this *stuff* you play with is going to be locked away for the remainder of your stay here."

She carried his belongings over to the cabinet, shoved everything inside, then selected a key from the key ring on her belt. The lock made a brisk *snap!* and she turned around to begin her daily fussing with his bed, his blankets, and his food tray.

"I think she's dead anyway," Cobalt said as he watched his servant. "And that's all I really care about. Go ahead and keep my effects. I won't be needing them anymore. Now get out of my house!"

The servant appeared to be long-suffering and at her wits' end. She sighed and rolled her eyes. "Mr. Scott," she said, "this is not your house, okay? This is your hospital room. I am not a servant. My name is Nancy Rivas." She tapped her name badge. "See? I'm your nurse."

Cobalt glared murderously and pressed his lips into a bloodless line. They were always trying to trick him like this. He should have been used to it by now, but it infuriated him every time. "Shut up and give me my food," he said.

Nurse Rivas ignored him. She wrapped a blood pressure cuff around his scrawny upper arm. "Hold still!" she commanded.

He offered no further comment, but continued to stare at her while she took his vitals.

"Food service will be here in a little while," she told him in a guarded tone. "Now you stay put. Understand, Mr. Scott?" She pressed the TV remote into his liver-spotted hand. "Here's the remote. Your shows will be on soon."

"My name is not Scott," the old man said. "I am Arlo Cobalt. How many times must I tell you this?"

Ping! Nancy Rivas to ICU. Nancy Rivas, ICU, please.

"I have to go for now," she told her belligerent patient. "You behave yourself."

—◆◈◆—

Out of all the dementia patients in this section of the hospital, Mr. Scott was by far the most difficult. His mind was deteriorating, but the spark in his eyes spoke of something else, something keenly aware and potentially dangerous.

Nurse Rivas came by later, around the time Scott took his afternoon nap. Housekeeping was just finishing up in Room 195; a brunette girl with a mop and a bad case of acne hustled out of the room wearing a look of wide-eyed bewilderment.

"You okay, Tina?" Rivas said. "I know, he can be difficult. You'll get used to him. Let me guess: He called you a servant and told you to get out of his house, right?"

Tina's mouth dropped open, showing a wad of purple bubble gum resting on her back molars. "No, nothing like that," she replied in a low voice. "His name's Scott, right? Mr. Scott?"

"Yep. That's the name he's registered under, anyway."

"He's calling himself Arlo Cobalt."

"Yes, he does that. He also thinks there are people in the ceiling. He's harmless, Tina. Let it go." Rivas glanced at her watch. "Are we done here?"

"Yes, but—you know who Arlo Cobalt is, don't you?" Tina's hand tightened around the mop handle, while the other held tightly to something on a fine gold chain around her neck.

"No, I don't, and I really don't care. Probably a character from one of the shows he watches. Last week we had someone here who thought there was a mariachi band coming down the hall."

Tina blinked at her and rolled her gum to the other side of her mouth. "But..."

"Look, the point I'm trying to make is people do strange things when they get old, okay? Nothing to worry about. Besides, he only started calling himself Arlo Cobalt a couple weeks ago. He's been in here a long time, and up until then, he always referred to himself as

Mr. Scott. All his paper work matches up. I've seen his I.D. He's not Arlo Cobalt, okay?"

Tina clutched her mop handle and nodded.

"All right then. Continue with your work, Tina." She winked— very slightly. "Now it's *my* turn to see him."

Once Nurse Rivas had continued down the hall and disappeared into Room 195, Tina relaxed her hold on the piece of jewelry in her hand. She ran her thumb over the tiny gold pentagram in her palm, then she tucked it back into the collar of her navy blue scrub top.

"Deegie Tibbs is dead," Scott said casually when Rivas entered the room.

"That's too bad," Rivas said as she counted the pulse beats in his scrawny old wrist. "Was Deegie Tibbs a pet you used to have?"

Scott looked at her as if she'd gone insane. "Of course not!" he scoffed. "She was the unwholesome spawn of a White Witch and a Dark Witch. An abomination. I'm glad she's dead."

"That's not a nice thing to say, Mr. Scott," she said primly. "Would you like me to bring you something for sleep? You look tired."

The old man rolled his head back on his stack of pillows, a look of misery on his mummy-like face. "It would be the least you could do," he said bitterly. "You are, after all, my servant."

Rivas positioned her stethoscope over his bony chest, touching him as little as she could. The lungs were rattling more than ever; the heartbeat a little weaker, but still ticking along. She made a notation on his chart and doused her hands with sanitizing foam from the dispenser by the door.

"Very well, Mr. Scott, and remember: Your cabinet is locked now and your remote is next to you on the bed. You stay where you are and use the *call* button if you need me. Do not *yell* for me, understand?"

The old man nodded and closed his eyes.

"All right then," she said, gathering up her clipboard and stethoscope. "I'll be right back."

CHAPTER ELEVEN

When Deegie awoke, she was lying on her side, her cheek pressed against cold, pebbled ground. She saw boot tops and denim-clad legs, then she looked up into the faces of the Altman brothers, who were staring down at her.

"Oh, thank all the gods!" Deegie let her eyes slide shut again. Her head hurt; everything hurt. "But who... I heard..." She put her hands to her face and took several deep breaths. *Breathe in lavender, breathe in light. Breathe out pain, breathe out fright.* She remembered the calming mantra her mother had taught her years ago and repeated it in her mind.

"We lost a young man named Danny Q.," she heard her father's voice say.

A third pair of boots crunched in the gravel next to her head. Her nose wrinkled at the scent of the Underworld. Tiger grunted and rumbled somewhere outside, close to the entrance. She knew she was safe, but her heart clenched painfully at the news of Danny Q.

"I feel like... like it's my fault." Deegie whispered. She felt the hot sting of tears begin behind her eyelids.

"No, Bunny. It isn't. You know it isn't. People helped you because they cared. In a way, he died for his own lost family member, too. Cobalt destroyed many lives, and sometimes victories require sacrifice."

Someone was touching her face now, most likely Zach or Gilbert. Hands lifted her head, and something soft was placed between her cheek and the ground. She smelled Gilbert's nose-murdering body spray. His sweatshirt most likely.

"Where are the rest?" Each word was like a small rocket launching in her head. She squeezed her hands against her temples and groaned.

"They all went back to the house." Gilbert said. "We can pretty much bet that Cobalt will be sending us more visitors. It will be safer for them back there. You rest. We got 'em all."

Deegie felt herself sliding away from the fireball still going off in head, but something else pulled her back. She just needed to know one more thing, then she would surrender to two or three hours of blessed, pain-free unconsciousness right here on the floor of the cave.

"That dog," she hissed between pain-clenched teeth. "That big black dog..."

"Hush!" Her father's harsh bark lanced into her head like a knitting needle. "You rest now. That's all."

Deegie heard the unmistakable sound of snapping fingers, and blackness took over for a while.

When she came to, the Altmans were gone. A hot, heavy weight lay across one of her legs and pressed against her body: Tiger Spirit. She was warm and surprisingly comfortable lying here on the ground. Angry red filaments of pain still wove their way through her brain, but she felt somewhat better. She propped herself up on an elbow. There was only a tiny silver of light coming through the cave entrance. Moonlight? Was it night?

Her father sat on a rock at the back of the cave. He leaned forward, elbows on knees, chin in hands. He was staring at her.

"Well, well. Look who's awake," he said, and he got up from his rock and went to her.

"Dad," she said, and she reached for him instinctively. He pulled back, his eyes full of sorrow, and she remembered something about not being allowed to touch him.

Roland snapped his fingers and a green flame appeared over a scattering of pebbles. It gave off a lambent heat but did not scorch the ground. Deegie moved closer.

"Cold?" Roland moved closer himself, watching her face.

"No. I'm okay. Tiger's been keeping me warm."

"I'm a bit chilly," Roland said. He held his hand over the little green flame and snapped his fingers again. The fire doubled in size with a soft *whoosh*. "I'm more used to, ah, warmer climes." Roland smiled. The warming flame turned his white teeth green.

Deegie gazed at him. His eyes were identical to hers, the same ice-blue, yet she caught the occasional red flicker. They reminded her of opals. He was her father, yet—he wasn't. It was more than just his strange, red-speckled eyes. Something else was missing that used to be there before. Was he still human? Was he a demon?

"Dad, I'm really confused here," she said. "Are you… you're… dead, right?" Gods, but that sounded horrible.

"Ah, yes." Roland rubbed his palms together. Red sparks, tiny, like glitter, fell from his hands and sparkled on the ground. "We *do* need to have this conversation." He reached for the fire again. "Warm enough?"

Deegie nodded. "Yes, Dad." Tiger pressed against her back, supporting her weight and blocking the draft from outside. The odd little flame warmed her front, and her headache lessened another notch.

"Very well, then." Roland rubbed his hands together again and Deegie laughed a little at the glittery red sparks.

"The man you knew as Roland Tibbs, your father, is dead, yes. I look like him, I talk like him, but I am something else entirely. I am what was condemned to an eternity in the Underworld after I married your mother, and we had you. I still have the *memories* of Roland Tibbs, but I am not him. You understand, don't you?"

"No," Deegie said. "That's just—how can you be my dad and not my dad at the same time? I mean, should I even *call* you Daddy?"

"I would be hurt if you didn't," Roland said. "Of course I'm still your father—in a way." He spread his wide, expressive hands and shook his head firmly, as if he was putting the subject to the side for now.

"Are you... are you a demon? Is that what you are?" Deegie asked the question that had been plaguing her since being reunited with her father.

"We'll have to discuss this another day, my dear. I don't want to trouble you with the details just yet; it would only cause you more pain and sadness, and I don't have a lot of time on the Earthly Plane. Hack can cover for me for a couple of days, but after that..." He ended his sentence with a shrug and pressed on. "I need you to accompany me to Pinecone Junction."

"What? Why? Damnit, Dad, I'm so confused right now!" The cave felt too warm now, and a dozen more questions log-jammed in her mind.

"I believe that's where we can find Cobalt. I need you to help me—how shall I put this—finish him off. End his career."

"Are you serious? Dad, I can't do that! I'm only good for two or three blasts! I'd be useless! You can take care of him by yourself... can't you?"

"No, I don't think so." Roland's eyes made their eerie opal flash, and when he grinned, Deegie noticed for the first time that the edges of his teeth were serrated, like tiny white steak knives. "He may be old and insane, but Arlo Cobalt will continue to be a danger to you, your friends, and any other witch affiliated with the Dark Ones. Just because he's a White Witch doesn't mean he's a *good* witch." He laughed and Deegie was just a little afraid of him then.

"It took ten witches, a Normal One, a spirit animal, and a condemned soul from the Underworld to defeat Cobalt's zombie army," Roland went on. "He is feeble, and clearly mad as a hatter. His conjurings are bizarre, but still we cannot underestimate him. But you and I can defeat him."

"*How*? I don't understand. This doesn't make any sense at all. Why can't *you* do it? Surely you're powerful enough. I mean, you're a... whatever it is you are now."

"Ssh, don't try to understand, just listen. Think back to how you felt when you found out what happened to your mother and me. You were grief-stricken, but you were enraged, weren't you? You wanted to find our killer and make him suffer a thousand slow deaths, didn't you?" Roland leaned forward as he spoke. His voice was flat and calm, a verbal ocean with no wind. Despite the flashes of red in his eyes, there was no warmth in them; no life, no soul.

"Daddy, don't... I don't want to think about that. This is getting really... I can't, Dad. Don't make me think about that night. Please don't!"

"But you *must*, Deegie!" Roland insisted. "I need you to remember that pain, that outrage, that white-hot need for revenge. You know that feeling, don't you?"

She hid her wet face in Tiger's fur and nodded.

"I do too." Roland said. "I still do. And Deegie, my darling, if we combine those feelings together, all that horror, all that outrage, we can create a spell so powerful it will reduce Cobalt to nothing more than a pile of smoldering refuse. All we need to do is pinpoint his exact location."

"But Dad, what about my Witch's Cramp? And the others? Why can't they help?" Deegie swiped at her wet cheeks with her fingers. He was right, though: That awful blend of horror and fear had never really left her heart. Many nights she'd lain awake wishing she could have the chance to stomp on the throat of her parents' killer. Maybe dig his eyes out of his still-living head and wear them on her fingers like olives.

"I've instructed them to stand by for now—we will most likely not need them—but I've had my servant install a portal in your house that will lead to wherever you and I might be. As for your Witch's Cramp, I promise you, Deegie, you won't feel a thing. I'll be directing the energy, not you. I'll take yours from you, but it won't hurt."

"Tiger will be with us though, right? I need him with me. I've been without him for so long." Warily, she pressed closer to her guardian.

"No, I'm afraid not. Tiger Spirit might cause, shall we say, *issues*. In his determination to protect you, there's a chance he would get in the way and hinder our mission. He will stay here and await your return. You won't be needing him this time."

"I'll always need him," she said, her voice cracking with emotion.

"Not this time," Roland repeated. He smiled again, and Deegie saw that his teeth had become longer and sharper. Dark hair sprouted on his cheeks and spread across his face. A long red tongue, longer than any normal human's, lolled from the side of his mouth.

Horrified, Deegie scrambled to her feet and almost stumbled against Tiger. "Dad? What the hell is *that*? Stop it! You're scaring me now!"

Roland laughed, and his voice was raw and rumbly. "Don't be frightened, Bunny. It's just one of the many things I've learned during my stay in the Underworld." He sat back on his heels and put his hands flat on the ground. Coarse, black hair raced up his arms. His ears traveled to the top of his head, where they became upright and pointed.

"It was you!" Fear yielded to wonderment, and Deegie gaped at the creature her quasi-father was becoming. "*You're* the black dog I saw!"

"Guilty as charged." Roland's voice was barely distinguishable as human now. An elegant tail burst from the seat of his pants and it waved back and forth, bringing up puffs of dust from the cave floor.

"I will be your faithful Hell Hound on our little excursion. *Hack! Hack! Bark! Barkbarkbark!*" His mouth was no longer capable of human speech, but his tail wagged furiously at Deegie. He gave her that distinctive canine grin as he barked for Mr. Hack.

A small portal opened at the back of the cave, and Mr. Hack stepped through on all fours. *Like a naked pink poodle squeezing through a doggie door,* Deegie thought, and she promised herself she'd laugh her ass off about it later. Aloud, she said, "Good evening, Mr. Hack."

"Evening," he replied curtly, not looking at her. "You'll be needing this." He thrust a battered canvas bag into her hands. Deegie noted with some alarm that it had the same cabbage rose print as her wallpaper back home.

"Inside are my master's leash, collar, identification tags, and literally anything else you might need. There are also some step-by-step instructions that I strongly encourage you to follow. Please note that my master's absence *will* be noticed sooner or later, and I suggest that you ensure his return in—"

"*Bark! Barkbark!*" Roland ended the discussion, and Hack dove back through the portal.

The creature that had once been her father looked up at her. His frosty blue eyes were the only feature she still recognized. Deegie reached for his sleek black head, then hesitated, remembering the rule about touching.

"How can you be my pet if I can't touch you? I'll need to put your collar on your neck, and then there's your leash, and—"

Her answer came in the form of a cold wet nose sliding across the back of her hand. Roland nudged the bag next, and made a puppy-like yip.

"Well, that answers that question. You have some pretty complicated rules, don't you?" Deegie wiped her damp hand on her jeans. "Gross, Dad."

He nudged the bag again, and she sat down on the rock Roland had recently vacated. She put the bag on her knees and opened the old-fashioned clasp. Her hand hesitated over the opening, then slipped inside.

The first thing she touched was a thick, cream colored envelope, just like the ones Moley gave her each month. It exuded the same heat that always accompanied the pay envelopes. Inside was an intricate hand-drawn map, a set of detailed instructions, and a generous amount of twenty-dollar bills folded over and held together with a silver money clip. Deegie unfolded the instructions and looked them over. The first step told her, in Moley's spidery handwriting, to *Collar and leash my master and the portal will appear at the back of the cave.* Deegie found the collar and leash in the bag, and she took them out and held them in front of Roland's furry black nose.

"Well," she said as she fastened them in place around Roland's neck, "looks like we're going on an adventure we'll never forget. If we live through it." Holding her father's leash in her hand, Deegie located the portal and stepped through.

CHAPTER TWELVE

Deegie felt a brief lurching sensation as she passed through into unknown territory with the huge black Hell Hound on a red leash. She had just enough time to realize she had no idea where she was going when the scent of fir needles hit her square in the face. She opened her eyes to brittle coastal wind and the distant fuss and boom of ocean waves. They stood on a hill. The Pacific fumed below them. The list of instructions was still warm in her hands, and Deegie lifted it again to read step two. Her hand shook, both from the cold and the weird frightened excitement that fizzed in her belly and tightened her throat.

Step Two: You are now in Pinecone Junction. Walk down the hill and turn left at the first road you see. Walk until you see the Seashell Lodge. A room has been reserved and paid for. Pick up the keys to the room, and wait there. Do not proceed with Step Three until the sun comes up.

Deegie scanned the list again and unfolded the map. It must have taken many hours to draw. The detail was exquisite. "*Moley* did this?" she asked aloud.

Roland barked.

"Gods, this is weird, even for me." Deegie said. "Okay, Dad. Here we go."

They threaded their way down the steep hill and turned left when they got to the road. There weren't many cars on the moonlit road, and Deegie was glad for this. The late hour would give her time to concoct a story to tell should anyone question the gigantic black dog walking beside her.

"You're an Alsatian hound," she said as they walked. "No, no, you're an Irish Wolfhound blend, or something like that. Okay?" Although she knew Roland couldn't reply in his hound form, Deegie talked to him anyway. The sound of her own voice was oddly soothing.

Roland had his nose to the road, testing the bouquet of scents there. He strained at his leash and Deegie tugged him back.

"Dad, why do you have to be a dog anyway? This is going to be a pain in the ass!"

"I can trace pick up a trace of Cobalt's scent this way," Roland said unexpectedly. "Hell Hounds have an extraordinary sense of smell. Better than any Earthly canine, in fact. It is also warmer for me this way."

Deegie looked down and screamed. Her father's Hell Hound body was now wearing his human head. He looked up at her calmly while his claws clicked along the pavement. "Why, what's the matter, my dear? You know I won't hurt you, and this is the only way I can chat with you."

"I know, I know, but Dad, what if someone sees you? Change back! That's just too weird!"

There was a muffled *foop* sound, and Roland wore his hound head once more. Still, he managed to give Deegie a pained look, and he lowered his nose to the ground to resume his olfactory exploration.

They didn't have to walk long before they spotted the Seashell Inn, a quaint twenty-room motel as pink and delicate as its name. The vacancy sign was lit, and underneath that, a smaller wooden sign read: PETS R WELCOME. There was a light on in the office and another sign propped up in the window sill which read: OPEN.

Checking in was, thankfully, without any further strangeness on the part of Deegie's Hell Hound father. The desk clerk was curious about the huge black dog in the lobby, however. "What kind of dog is that?" she asked as she slid Deegie's room key across the counter.

"Huh? Oh, he's uh… um… like, part Alsatian hound and part Irish wolfhound, I think. He's a good boy." She picked up her room key and hid her reddening cheeks behind a springy lock of hair.

"Come on, Dad," Deegie said, giving the leash a tug. She instantly regretted her choice of words. *Dad? Oh, damn. I had to go and say that, didn't I?* She hustled towards the door, groaning inwardly.

"His name's Dad?" the clerk chuckled behind her. "That's cute. Enjoy your stay!"

Deegie waved over her shoulder, the bag tucked under her arm.

Once behind the locked door of their pastel-colored, faintly mildew-scented room, Deegie fell backward on the bed and let out all her pent-up energy in a prolonged sigh. Roland turned around three times and curled up nose to tail in the corner.

Deegie was hungry. She remembered Moley's words about the cabbage rose bag, and she had a feeling all she needed to do to silence her grumbling belly was look inside. After all, it was supposed to hold "literally everything" she might need. *Sure wish I had a Bomber Burger Deluxe and some fries,* she thought hopefully.

She could smell her meal before she even opened the clasp: a double cheeseburger with extra onions, a chocolate milkshake, and a large order of fries. She dug the food out of the bag, marveling at her good fortune and wondering if she got to keep the miraculous bag as a parting gift when this was all over.

"Hey, Dad, I bet if you looked in here, you'd find something good to eat, too." She laughed. "Maybe some jerky snacks or soup bones! Hey, I wonder if there'll be jammies and hot chocolate in there at bedtime. This is the most amazing thing I've ever seen! Do I get to keep this bag after all is said and done?"

When he didn't reply—through neither words nor barks—Deegie peered over the edge of the bed, wondering where her shaggy black father had gone. "Dad?"

Roland still lay where he had collapsed when they'd first entered. His breathing was slow and deep, and his paws twitched erratically, as if he were dreaming of running.

Poor Daddy, Deegie thought as she squeezed ketchup over her fries. *He must have been up all night because of me.* She wolfed her meal in silence, wondering what the magic bag would conjure up next. When she was finished, she stretched out on the bed and read from the list.

Step Three: In step three you will investigate near a red-brick post office. This is where I lost the trail; I do not have the olfactory skills of my master. I am sure he will pick up the scent immediately. You have until this time tomorrow night to pinpoint Cobalt's location and put him out of commission. Once this is complete, text SOS to UWHOT to open the escape portal. A cell phone has been provided for you. You will find it in the bag.

Deegie didn't want to sleep. She trusted her father, despite what he was now. She knew he wouldn't let anything happen to her. But this… this *mission*, as Moley called it—was it really necessary? After all, Cobalt had been ancient eleven years ago, when his murderous hate had torn her family apart. Surely it wouldn't be long until nature ran its course. Did they really need to kill an old, sick man?

She brought her mind back to that awful night. *Am I horrible for being able to do that so well?* she wondered. How many hours had she stayed in that closet, hidden away in the darkness until Moley found her? How many months did it take until the sounds of her parents' murder stopped replaying in her head? And the other witches, her new friends. Their suffering mattered too, and Arlo Cobalt was the cause of *all* of it. Deegie located that tender spot in her heart that respected all life, and she locked it away in a temporary mental holding cell. This was no time for her usual gentleness. Of course this man deserved to die, and if it was evil to think so, then she'd be happy to spend eternity with her father as punishment.

The net of pent-up anxiety and trepidation began to ease, and Deegie finally allowed herself to sink into the crackly pillow and stiff, scratchy blanket. Outside the window, the birds were just beginning to fuss and stir. She might be able to get an hour's worth of sleep in before their search for the park and the brick post office.

I can't wait to see his face she thought, just before she drifted off. *Can't wait to see the look in his eyes when we finally meet face to face.*

Something wet swiped across her nose a short while later. Deegie smelled rotten meat and swamp water. She sat up, grimacing in disgust, and rubbing a bed sheet over her face. "Dad! *Gross!*"

Roland barked and ran towards the door with his leash in his mouth.

"Are you serious?" She gazed at him blearily, her face creased in sleep. "Can't you just shape-shift to a human form and use the bathroom like anyone else?"

Roland barked again, holding the leash in his teeth, and the cell phone bleated out a text message alert from the gaping mouth of the bag.

"Shit. All right." She sat up and put her socks on inside out. "Everyone hold their horses!"

While Roland sniffed the ground and peed on the bushes behind the hotel, Deegie read the text message: *Time to get up! Time to get moving! The countdown to the annihilation begins! Please see that my master is allowed adequate time in the trees. More to follow.*

"Now *that* was unnecessary," Deegie grumbled aloud. Realizing she had let Roland run loose without his leash, she cupped a hand around her mouth and shouted, "Dad! Get out of the bushes! We have to go!"

Someone giggled, and Deegie glanced left. A little girl stood a few doors down, holding a toy poodle at the end of a leash. "Dad!" The girl bent double in fit of laughter. "Your dog's name is Dad!"

"Yeah," Deegie muttered as she watched Roland come bounding through the forest. "I need to change that."

By following Moley's map, Deegie and Roland located the red brick library. The park was across the street. Barbeque grills and picnic tables hibernated under a quilt of snow. Their hunched, white shapes looked like bizarre frost creatures.

"I wonder if this is the only park." Deegie was slightly out of breath from their brisk morning walk. She'd had to remind Roland to slow down more than once.

"This is the only park that matters." Roland's voice echoed in the garbage can he was exploring. He was wearing his human head again, and Deegie turned away.

"Dad, please. That's so creepy." She whipped her head around, making sure no one else was in sight. "Besides, we don't have time for you to be sniffing the garbage."

"How else am I supposed to talk to you?" Roland backed out of the garbage can and waved his tail at her. Although his head was now human, he continued to sniff the air and the frozen sidewalk. "And besides, I'm sniffing the garbage, as you put it, for a reason: I smell Cobalt."

"What? You mean he was here?" She looked down at Roland, forcing herself to focus on his face only. "How could we get that lucky?"

"No, not Cobalt himself. Someone who's been near him, a family member, or a friend. They've thrown away a tissue or something, and recently, too." He thrust his head back into the garbage can. Vigorous sniffing sounds ensued. "I smell hospital too, and *(sniff-sniff)* a woman, maybe a nurse. I just need to pick up the scent on the sidewalk, and I think we can—someone's coming." Roland stuck his head back in the garbage can, and Deegie heard the *foop!* sound of his head returning to that of a dog.

An elderly couple ambled past; the woman glared at Deegie from under crookedly drawn brows. One arched higher than the other, giving her a perplexed look. The old folks shuffled off, cackling to each other in a language Deegie didn't recognize.

She looked down at Roland. His nose scooted over the ground as he reached the end of his leash. His head shot up, as if he'd spotted something in the distance. He barked and lunged; Deegie's shoulder joint strained.

"Ow! Shit! Be careful, Dad!"

Roland's vigorous tugging pulled her through a deep puddle of slush as they crossed the park. Deegie's feet were instantly soaked, but she saved her breath for running. She could grouse about it later. She was towed along the sidewalk towards the park's back entrance, where Roland abruptly dropped to his haunches. The park's back entrance was on St. Helens Road, next to a tobacconist and a menswear shop. Across from that was another red brick building. This one had white trim and a white sign creaking back and forth on a black wrought iron frame. Pinecone Junction General Hospital.

"He's in there? Cobalt's in *there?*" Deegie wiped her forehead with her gloved fingers. The dash through the park had been unexpected, but exhilarating.

Roland dipped his head in what passed for a nod. He lifted his snout and whined.

"Do we go in and pretend to be visitors?" Deegie kept her voice low, and there were no other people in sight, but it still felt strange talking to her father in his Hell Hound guise. The cell phone buzzed against her leg and she dug it out of her pocket. Another helpful text message from Moley had the answer to her question: *Once my master has found Cobalt's hideout, you must wait for him at the park while he scouts the area under the spell of invisibility. He will contact you when he is ready for your assistance.*

"All right, then." Deegie reached down and unclipped the leash from Roland's collar. "Go on ahead, Dad. Find that bastard. I'll wait for you here."

Roland dashed away, his huge paws making divots in the snow. He ran halfway across the road and vanished. Only the disturbance of the snow indicated his progress toward the hospital. Deegie stood and stared, fascinated by the sight of the massive canine footprints that seemed to appear by themselves. She'd always wanted to learn the spell of invisibility, but since it was a spell that required a huge amount of energy, she doubted she had the ability. Her father had done it with ease; he hadn't even broken his stride.

Once she was back in the park, Deegie cleared a butt-sized patch of snow from one of the picnic benches. After a quick look around, she snapped her fingers and whispered *"Calefactare!"* Bright orange flame lit up the exposed wooden bench, and the air turned sharp with the primal smell of camp fire. Deegie's head tightened in warning, but it was worth it. She sat down on the dry, cozy bench to await further instruction.

CHAPTER THIRTEEN

The witches assembled once again at 14 Fox Lane. The mood was somber and dark, in sharp contrast to the bright winter day. Gilbert carefully positioned a length of firewood on the andiron, making sure both ends hung over evenly. He yanked his hands away from the awakening fire before his arm hairs began to curl, then went to sit by himself in the recliner next to the boarded-up window. He picked up a cup of gone-cold coffee and swallowed some without tasting it. He could still hear Flower's voice coming from the kitchen, where she'd taken over and was baking something in Deegie's oven. The others were in there too, listening to the old hippie woman with rapt attention. She went on and on, in great detail, about what steps should be taken next. Her voice was annoying. Gilbert hated it when people just took over a situation like that. He'd had everything well in hand, thank you very much.

It wasn't right to leave Deegie on the hill like that, even if it was with her father. They should have *all* come down. Deegie was one bad-ass witch, but she was a *disabled* bad-ass witch. Gilbert didn't see the logic in taking her along on such an important mission, but he wasn't about to argue with a guy like Roland. Gilbert scrubbed his fingers on his pant legs, leaving black smudges from the fireplace. Cold air worked itself around the boarded-up window and whirled across the floor. He decided he would call to get it fixed as soon as this latest ordeal was over. It was the least he could do after allowing Deegie to be left up on the hill, stuffed into a crack in a rock.

A stealthy shuffle and thump from upstairs reminded Gilbert of something else: Lisbet the ghost had roamed the house all night, searching for her missing friend. Earlier that morning, Bast had shredded the lacy curtains in the kitchen window because someone had forgotten to feed him.

Funny how things always fell apart when Deegie was gone.

Once he reached the parking lot of Pinecone Junction General Hospital, Roland resumed his human form. Still under the spell of invisibility, he waited outside the door until another visitor went inside, then he slipped in after him. At the end of a short entry hall was a lobby with a brown corduroy couch and a dusty plastic ficus. Roland slid along the wall, noiseless and unseen, and waited for someone to open the door next to the reception desk.

He didn't have to wait long.

A grey-haired woman in green scrubs opened the door from the other side. She held it open with her hip while she scanned the clipboard in in hand. Roland saw his chance and slipped through undetected. Once he entered the maze of hallways, Roland dropped to all fours and resumed his Hell Hound form.

Still unseen and completely unnoticed, he lowered his nose to the floor and picked up the trail again. Little more than a whisper of breeze, Roland followed the nurse who had walked through the park on her break. If he accompanied her on her rounds, he'd be seeing Arlo Cobalt soon enough. His thick tail gonged against a passing food cart, but of course the nurse saw nothing out of the ordinary when she turned around. She scowled at the food service girl anyway and turned the corner with the enormous invisible Hell Hound right behind her.

Cobalt's scent was stronger now. The scents of insanity and despair burned their way into Roland olfactory gland; it was a struggle to keep from howling with rage. The need for vengeance overpowered him and made him tremble as he walked briskly along behind the nurse. She paused in front of Room 195 and scribbled something on her clipboard. She went inside and Roland followed her.

Cobalt was smaller than Roland remembered. He was withered and shrunken, his skull clearly delineated beneath the thin skin of his nearly hairless head. His eyes were still bright and alert, however, and they widened when he caught sight of the nurse. He grinned at the empty space behind her, and Roland had the oddest feeling Cobalt could see him. This crazy old man couldn't see through an invisibility spell, could he? Roland tucked himself behind the room's only chair so he wouldn't trip the nurse.

"Is someone else in here with you, my dear?" The old man's voice rose tremulously from the mound of white sheets and pillows.

"Nope. Just me, Mr. Scott." The nurse took her stethoscope from around her neck and plugged it into her ears. "Go ahead and sit up for me, and I'll check your lungs."

"I had the strangest sensation someone else was in here, too." Cobalt did as he was told; he sat up and leaned forward. "Hell, I'm old. I'm probably still asleep."

While the nurse busied herself checking the old man's vitals, he continued to stare into the space behind the chair. His smile was slow and reptilian.

He certainly does NOT see me! Roland thought as he stared back. He made sure his expression was fierce, just in case. He stole out from behind the chair and lifted his lip in a threatening snarl. *You know I'm here, don't you, old timer? You might not be able to see me, but you know I'm here.*

Cobalt continued to stare and smile, seemingly at nothing, and his nurse wore a troubled expression as she made notations on her clipboard. Roland had a hunch that Cobalt was not long for this world. If he still wanted to be the one to take the old man out of commission, he'd better hurry.

Deegie saw the footprints her father made in the snow before he materialized in front of her. Suddenly he was visible, sitting on the ground at her feet with his long tongue lolling from his mouth. He barked, urgently, and Deegie sighed.

"Dad, can you *please* be a person when we discuss this? Just be my dad for a little while, okay?"

Foop! Humanoid Roland knelt on all fours, with slush seeping into his pant legs and shirt cuffs. "As you wish, Bunny," he said, rising to his feet. "Although my fur coat would be a better choice in this climate."

Deegie kicked more snow off the bench and warmed it as she had done before. She inhaled deeply, savoring the brief campfire smell. "There you are, Dad. Okay, now where is he? I mean, you found him, right?"

Roland sat and rubbed his hands together briskly. "Indeed I did," he said, his face grim. "He is very near. I saw him. I can't get the stench of him out of my nose." He patted the rapidly cooling wooden bench and added, "And no more spells for you, missy. Not even little ones. The last thing we need is for you to get an attack of Witch's Cramp."

"Okay, okay." Deegie made an impatient sweeping-aside gesture with her hand, "Is he ancient and sick like we thought?"

"Yes, quite. He is a withered hunchbacked gnome of a man. He appeared harmless enough until I saw his eyes. His body is failing him; I saw a look of great concern on his nurse's face as she examined him. His mind is affected as well, but remember—that old man brought nearly two dozen dead people back to life just the other day."

"Dad, I really don't feel right about this. We should have brought some of the others with us. We can't do this by ourselves... can we?"

Roland conjured a miniature fireball, similar to the ones in the cave. It hung in mid-air in front of him. He held his hands in front of it, welcoming its warmth. "Of course we can," he said. "The nurse gave him a sleeping pill. We'll just do away with him while he's asleep. Quick and painless."

"What? Quick and painless? It wasn't quick and painless for you and Mom!" Deegie's face darkened with anger.

Roland seemed thrilled by her outburst. "Yes!" he exclaimed, "there it is!" He clapped his hands together and extinguished the fireball. "That anger, Deegie! That fury! Remember to bring that anger up and hold onto it."

"Can't we just, you know, disconnect his machines? Pull the plug and let him die on his own?" Deegie felt it again, that tiny stab of shame at the thought of killing a sick old man. It vanished as quickly as it came, and she forced herself to remember what a monster Cobalt really was.

"He's not attached to any machines. Not that I can see, anyway." Roland shook his head firmly. "No. An ordinary murder won't do; we are not ordinary people and neither is he. A single jolt will do the trick—a concentrated blast of pure hate. It will stop his heart just as he once stopped mine and that of my wife. You can do this, Deegie. You *are* half Dark one, remember."

Deegie nodded, looked at the snow between her boots, and sighed. "I know, Dad. And you're right. I feel that need for revenge. It gets huge sometimes. Not only that, I'm sick of having to be careful all the time, like I'm in witness protection or something." She smiled bitterly. "Besides, he might get better and go on to kill more of us if we let him live. I don't know about you, but I don't think I could forgive myself if I allowed that to happen."

"Ah, now you're making sense!" Roland stood up and winced as the cold chewed through the thin leather of his boots. "Come on then, let's get this done. It will be quick, I promise."

Deegie rose to her feet and checked the cell phone. No further comments from Moley, but that was all right. The rest of the mission was pretty self-explanatory: sneak into a hospital, murder an old man, then get the hell out. Got it.

"You will be under the protection of my invisibility spell," Roland said. "No one will be able to see either of us. We don't even need to show ourselves if you don't want to."

She considered this briefly. "No," she said. "I want him to see me. I want to see the look in his eyes before we end his career."

Roland laughed heartily; the sunlight glinted off his serrated teeth. "Deegie, my dear," he said, "your Dark side is showing!"

He pointed at the leash in her hand. "Get ready to go for a casual stroll with your trusty hound," he said. "And when I become invisible, you will too. Just follow my lead."

"All right." She waited for a man and his mutt to pass then nodded and held up the leash. "Go ahead and change. I'm ready."

She closed her eyes and turned away until she heard energetic canine panting and felt the lash of a heavy tail against her leg. Deegie fastened the collar and leash around Roland's neck, then let him lead her back through the park and across the street. He towed her around to the rear entrance of Pinecone Junction General Hospital, and then planted himself in the middle of the sidewalk. He turned his head to look at her, and blinked his eyes thrice. Deegie could have sworn he was smiling at her.

She felt a jolt, then a full-body tingle as she disappeared. Deegie lifted her hand and waved it before her eyes, but she saw nothing but the red brick wall of the hospital. Looking down where her feet should be showed her nothing but the icy sidewalk. Roland was nowhere in sight.

"Dad? Am I gone? This feels weird. I changed my mind. Please change me back!" Her voice fluttered on the edge of panic, and she dropped the leash.

"Shh! You're okay, Bunny. I take it this is the first time you've experienced an invisibility spell?"

His voice was an unexpected whisper in her left ear and she drew back with a startled gasp. "Where are you? I *hate* this!"

"Easy now," Roland's disembodied voice was on the right now. "It will take a few minutes to get used to. You're still very much there, you're just… unseen."

The air in front of her took on a brief shimmering quality, the way it did when she knew Tiger Spirit was near. "Daddy? Is that you?"

"Of course," Roland replied, a hint of a chuckle in his voice. "Listen up now. Go straight down the main hallway when you go through the door. Be careful not to make any noise. Remember: you're unseen, not unheard. Follow the hallway and take the very last right, just before the exit sign. He's in the last room on the left, number 195. We'll materialize at the foot of his bed. We will speak to him if you wish, but psychically, silently, so as not to attract attention before our mission is done. I will give you the brief ability to do so. Then I will conduct my fatal spell. Questions?"

Although he couldn't see her, Deegie shook her head. "No, Dad," she said. "I trust you. Let's just do this, okay?"

"All right, then. Bring up your fierceness, Deegie. Get it to boiling. I'll need everything you can muster."

The rear door swung open. It was strange to see it do that without a visible human to assist. Deegie stepped inside. She had long hated the smell of a hospital. An old one like this smelled even worse: disinfectant spray, rubbing alcohol, stale coffee, and underneath all that, the slightest hint of mildew and decaying brick. It was the smell of despair and of lives drawing to a close.

Ahead of her, the air shimmered again, and Deegie doubled her pace. As she followed her invisible father, she allowed herself to revisit the night of her parents' murder. Once again she unlocked the dam holding back that torrent of tooth-gnashing, soul-crushing emotions. She encouraged the rising flood of heartbreak mixed with rage. Her throat tightened; her jaw clenched. By the time she reached Room 195, she was holding back shrieks of rage.

Her father waited for her at the foot of a standard hospital bed. He was fully in human form, his long black cloak flowing to his ankles. His eyes blazed with the crimson fire of the Underworld. When Deegie reached his side, she felt a buzzing sensation at the base of her skull, and she was visible again. She stood next to her father, their shoulders nearly touching, and together they stared down at the man in the bed. Arlo Cobalt barely made a lump under the thin hospital blanket. His naked head made a slight dent in the pillow. His eyes were closed in slumber.

Roland waved a hand across Deegie's face, his fingers barely grazing her cheeks. The top of her head clenched painlessly. In her mind she heard her father's voice: *"Psychic speech will come naturally to you now. Believe me, he'll hear us."*

Deegie gazed at her father in wonderment as he spoke to her without moving his mouth. *"Let's wake this bastard up, then,"* she replied, and she felt a skittering sensation run across her scalp as she transmitted the thought to Roland.

She curled her fingers around the safety rail of Cobalt's bed and gripped it tightly. The old man in the bed looked tiny and harmless. Could she do this? A wave of hatred washed the question aside. Of course she could. He wasn't a man; he was sheer evil disguised as good. He was the maniac who had murdered her parents. Not even her father's apostasy had saved them. The need for revenge rose higher, burning like acid. Deegie's upper lip curled in a sneer.

Roland reached up and pulled the privacy curtain around the bed, shielding curious eyes from what was about to transpire.

"*Cobalt!*" The sound of her father's unspoken voice boomed in Deegie's head. Cobalt's withered form stirred.

"*Cobalt! I know you're awake! Open your eyes and look at me!*"

The old man raised his eyelids. A slow, sickly smile widened his gaunt cheeks. "Roland Tibbs. You're supposed to be dead," he croaked. "I thought I caught the stench of Dark Witch earlier."

"*Ah, but sadly I am no longer Roland.*" Roland's voice was silky with danger. He moved to Cobalt's side, motioning for Deegie to follow. "*Thanks to you, I am now known as Klaa, General of the Underworld.*"

"Impressive title, that." Cobalt managed a thick, phlegmy chuckle. "I offer you congratulations on your impressive new... incarnation." His gaze slid over to Deegie, and his thin-lipped smile faltered and died.

"Deegie Tibbs." Cobalt spat out her name as if it left a foul taste on his tongue. "You're supposed to be dead as well. I've already killed both of you. Bah!" His hand trembled and lifted a few inches from the bed as he tried to wave them away. "I'm dreaming this. It's those damn pills they keep giving me." But his eyes told another story; they were quick and sly and knowing. Cobalt was like an ancient timber rattler, coiling for the strike.

Deegie was fairly bursting with the need for revenge. Rage and hatred boiled in her belly. Yes, this was the right thing to do. It would be a pleasure to watch the old fart die.

"*I must admit, I'm impressed,*" Roland said in this new and fantastic manner of communication. "*I never thought a witch as old and feeble as you could conjure such an impressive*—ahem—*army. It's a shame it wasn't very effective.*"

Cobalt regarded the two of them with his half-lidded gaze. The dry tip of his tongue poked out and rasped along even drier lips. "You could at least fetch an old man a glass of water before you murder him in his bed," he said.

Deegie sent a harsh, barking laugh into Cobalt's brain. "*I wouldn't spit in your mouth if you were dying of thirst!*" She hurled the thought-form at the old man. A scattering of red sparks escaped from her fingertips and drifted down to the floor.

Cobalt infuriated her even further by laughing at her. His shrill cackle sent another bolt of hatred racing through her psyche.

"Your mother died a little too quickly for my taste, Ms. Tibbs," he said. "But she screamed gloriously, don't you think?"

More sparks erupted from Deegie's fingertips as she fought to contain her fury. They fell to the floor in smoking crimson clusters. "*You bastard,*" she whispered. "*Oh, you slimy son of a bitch.*"

Roland looked at her sharply. He shook his head in an almost imperceptible movement. *Not yet,* his expression told her. *Not yet...*

"But I suppose my glory days are over now, aren't they?" Cobalt went on with a theatrical sigh. "Alas, the assassin is about to become the assassinated, it would appear." He rolled his head over the thin pillow and focused his gaze on Roland.

"It's a damn shame I couldn't have exterminated your half-breed brat, Tibbs. Tell me, would she have been reincarnated as Underworld trash as well?"

Deegie clutched the bedrail again and squeezed it hard. "*Daddy, do it! Kill him! What are you waiting for?*"

She moved closer to the being she still called her father. His expression was serene, almost amused. He raised his left hand and hovered it over Deegie's head, ready to draw out her white-hot fury and combine it with his own. He held his right hand over Cobalt's bald pate, where the fatal energy blend would ultimately be directed. *"I'm getting a little tired of your insults, Cobalt. Deegie is too, I'll wager. It's a shame that's all you can seem to muster after the valiant fight you've put up."* Roland lowered his hand to the top of Cobalt's head.

"Time to go, Cobalt. Tell me, where do you think you'll go after Deegie and I have extinguished your miserable life? Are you absolutely sure that your so-called crusade has been righteous enough to grant your immortal soul immunity from the Underworld?"

Cobalt did not reply to Roland's question. Instead, his bloodless lips moved soundlessly, as if he were in silent prayer. His eyes grew huge and glassy. His gnarled hand jerked and trembled as he lifted it from the bed, and he raised his head to look at Roland.

"A demon's heart," Cobalt wheezed. "Did you know that the heart of a demon can be used for emergency magic? And really, Tibbs, when one's immortal soul is banished to the Underworld, wouldn't that make one... a demon?"

His knobby old hand, previously laboring to rise from the bed, shot upwards with surprising speed and force. It hovered in the air, directly in front of Roland's chest, wavering back and forth like an ancient cobra.

Deegie drew in a breath, held back a scream. *"Daddy, watch out!"* Something tightened in her mind at the force of her thought-form.

As Roland brought his spell hand up to release a counter blow, the bony tips of Cobalt's fingers clustered together in a point and drove directly into Roland's chest.

CHAPTER FOURTEEN

When the fire in the old field stone fireplace began to die down, Gilbert rose to poke at the coals. It just felt better in here, and it gave him something to do while he awaited further word about Deegie. The fireplace poker was still outside, lying in a snowbank where Zach had abandoned it after the battle with the zombie-crows. He used the shovel instead and reminded himself to fetch the poker from outside before Deeg came home. The place was trashed again too; he'd have to get started on that soon.

An odd fluttering in the chimney caught his attention as he tried to coax more flame out of the embers. Gilbert stopped and frowned. A bat, perhaps? A bit of paper? He craned his neck, trying to look up the chimney without sticking his head inside the fireplace and roasting it off. Something plummeted down the sooty stone tub and landed on the andiron.

It might have been a huge moth, or an overgrown dragonfly; its wings incinerated too quickly to tell. It had a thick, grub-like body that writhed and sizzled in the heat from the fire.

"What the *hell?*" Gilbert prodded the insectile thing with the blade of the fireplace shovel. He flipped it over. Its legs were reduced to charred bone, and that couldn't be right. Insects didn't have bones.

The creature waved the stumps of its wings. It wailed, loud and shrill, as its head burst into flame. The moth-like fizz burned away, revealing a tiny, screaming human skull. Another one swooped down the chimney. This one managed to pull up in time to avoid the embers, and it left the fireplace in a cloud of ash and soot. Gilbert backed up, keeping a steady eye on the insect-thing hovering in front of him. He cocked the shovel over his shoulder like Zach had done with the poker and waited for his chance to clobber it.

"Hey! You guys might want to come in here!" Gilbert yelled for the others as he swung and missed. "Hey! You guys! A little help here?"

This one had the face of an old woman. Its diminutive mouth, toothless and lined with fine wrinkles, screamed a torrent of obscenities at Gilbert as it dodged the fireplace shovel. Six human legs, the size of wooden match sticks, were arranged along the furry abdomen. A thick stinger spouted from its ass-end. Vicious green liquid oozed from the tip.

The bug-creature exploded in a brilliant flash of light; hot bug guts splattered Gilbert's face.

Nix leapt in front of him, holding her still-smoking wand aloft. The other witches followed, ready to face this onslaught and crying out in disgust at what they saw.

Flower pointed toward the fireplace. "There's more of them! Get that fire going again!"

A half-dozen flying horrors rocketed into the living room, bringing a grey billow of fireplace ash with them. Their horrifyingly human faces were of an assortment of races and ages. They spewed curses and vile insults from their mouths as they swooped and dove at the witches with their hooked, dripping stingers.

Zach snatched a stack of junk mail from the coffee table and flung it into the fireplace. Flames burst into life. More insect-people swarmed down the chimney and were disabled by the multicolored flames rising from a blazing catalogue. Next, he grabbed a length of firewood from the stack by the hearth and hurled it onto the blazing junk mail. A fountain of sparks rose up. Singed and dying insect-people rained down. He shoved in more paper and kindling; thick, yellow flames roared. "Got it!" he yelled.

He spun away from the fireplace just as one of the insectile horrors came in for a landing on the top of Rosenstraum's head. The big man turned in an ever-widening circle, bellowing in pain and protest as he slapped and tugged at the freak of nature that clung to his head. The creature's tiny hands grabbed and clutched at his hair. Its hooked stinger plunged up and down. Franklin, one of the younger witches, fired off a well-aimed bolt, and the creature detonated in a spray of yellow sparks and green pureed guts. Rosenstraum crumpled to the floor, his face already swelling.

The witches disposed of the rest of the insect-people, but not without a great deal of effort. Cobalt's latest batch of foot soldiers were small and swift, making them difficult targets. The once tidy, eclectically decorated living room was splattered and streaked with clots of greenish gore and littered with tiny charred bones. They ran as a group to the fallen Rosenstraum; Flower dropped to her knees at his side.

"Witches!" she called out. "Send white light! Everything you have! Right here!"

She raised her arms above her head and held her cupped palms about a foot apart. The witches raised their spell hands; Nix and Gilbert held wands. They sent out six beams of brilliant white light, aiming them directly at the space between Flower's hands.

Zach pressed against the wall and kept himself out of the way while he looked on. A white glowing ball took shape between Flower's hands. She let it grow to the size of a beach ball, then nodded at Gilbert and the other witches. They shut off their beams at once, then stepped back so the elder witch could work her magic. She lowered the ball, gently and reverently, until it touched the fallen man's forehead.

Rosenstraum shifted and moaned. He was still alive; there was still hope. His face, bathed in white light, was a terrible thing to look upon. The virulent poison the bug-things had injected into his head was fast acting. His face was swelling to grotesque proportions, and his body twitched as the ball of light seemed to liquefy and seep into his mouth and nose. The giant clawed at the air and tried to sit up.

"Breathe it in," Flower urged softly. "Let it enter you!"

A thick gurgling sound rose in Rosenstraum's throat and he fell back to the floor. The elder witch frowned. Tired grey light drifted out of Rosenstraum's mouth and dissolved into nothingness.

"I'm afraid we're too late," Flower muttered. She took off her multicolored pashmina and covered Rosenstraum's face.

"Cobalt's getting stronger," Gilbert said as he rose to his feet. "How is that possible? I thought the bastard was old and sick!"

"I wonder if…" Nix swallowed hard and started over. "Do you suppose Ms. Tibbs and her father made it? I mean it's possible they're—"

"Enough!" Zach stepped away from the wall and moved closer to the group. "Enough," he said again, holding up both hands. "I know I'm the Normal One here, but please, don't talk like that. Deegie's tough. She's a bad ass. She's fine."

Nix's eyes travelled to the window behind Zach, and her mouth dropped open. "Save it for later, Normal," she said, pointing. "Look!"

The window's top pane was still intact, allowing them to see an approaching swarm of the insect people. They made fast-moving shadows over the snow. A couple of them clung to the side of the house already. They had angry human faces and peered through the glass at the witches, shrieking and cursing and beating on the window with tiny, insistent fists. More of them landed on the roof. Their wings made horrid buzzing sounds, and their naked human feet skittered over the shingles as they searched for another way in. Their muffled voices shrieked and chattered.

Something tapped against the square of cardboard covering the broken bottom window. A hooked stinger punched through, a drop of venom glistening at its tip. It withdrew, leaving a round hole. Fingers, no bigger than a grain of rice, appeared around the edge of the hole. They tugged. The hole widened. A miniature human face with faceted insectile eyes peered through the rip in the cardboard. It grinned at the witches, then shrieked with laughter as it tried to force its way inside.

—◦✦◦—

Roland's body stiffened; a look of utter surprise crossed his face, and he struggled to form words. Cobalt's hand was mired to the wrist in his chest.

"A demon's heart," Cobalt purred again. His eyes rolled in his shrunken face and he smiled his jack-o-lantern smile. "I call upon my army of flying death! Fly, my faithful ones! Pierce their filthy skins with your lances and inject them with your venom!" Spittle flew from his lips as he followed up with an old man's shrill cackle.

Deegie realized she'd been dragging her hands down her face in silent horror. She composed herself enough to yank her spell hand away and fire a bolt at Cobalt. *"Stop it!"* Sparks crackled from her fingertips as she screamed at him with her mind. *"Let him go!"*

The look Cobalt gave her was almost apologetic. "Dear, stupid, half-breed bitch," he said. "He's dead anyway, isn't he? I'm simply sending him back where he belongs. But don't worry, love. You'll be joining him soon."

Roland writhed and clutched at the withered arm that had impaled him.

Cobalt smirked. The tendons in his branch-like arm stood out as he tightened the fist buried in Roland's chest.

She could tell her father was screaming, but she couldn't hear the sound. Deegie fell to her knees, unable to tear her eyes away.

"Daddy! No!" She didn't know if she'd screamed the words aloud or in her head. She didn't care. Red lightening shot from her hand as she fired at Cobalt again.

He raised his other hand and deflected her blast with an almost casual ease. He squeezed Roland's heart harder.

Roland had ceased his silent screaming. He hung limply at the end of Cobalt's arm. His body began to fade, as if he were made of smoke and was slowly blowing away. He turned his head to look at Deegie, and right before he disappeared completely, he winked.

Cobalt pulled his hand back and smirked at the horrified young woman next to his bed. "Now then," he said, "time to finish taking out the trash." He cocked his arm, taking aim at Deegie.

She didn't bother with defensive magic. She swatted his hand away, slapped him across the face, and seized his grizzled throat with both hands. "What did you do to him?" Her voice was a deadly whisper in his hairy ear. "What did you do to my dad?" She readied herself to spring onto the mattress and squeeze the last undeserved breath out of him.

There was no fear showing on Cobalt's face, only insanity. He grinned up at Deegie but did not reply. She caught a flicker of motion at the corner of her eye: Cobalt's hand moving once again. A comet of hot blue flame missed her head by inches and slammed into her shoulder. She flew across the bed and crashed into the nightstand, taking the bed curtain with her. Cobalt fired again. The bolt sizzled overhead, and Deegie's nose filled with the stench of burning hair.

"Deegie Tibbs!" Cobalt boomed. His voice held a power that hadn't been there before, and he sat up straight and swung his legs over the side of the bed. "Did you really think you could defeat me? You won't make that mistake again, will you?" He stood and advanced towards her.

Deegie scrambled backward, trying to dodge Cobalt's bolts and get up at the same time. The cord to the room's phone snagged on her ankle and the instrument fell to the floor with a bang and a muffled *ding!* Her hands scrabbled over the floor, searching for anything that could be used as a weapon. She guessed that she had another blast left in her, possibly two. But to do so would surely bring on the Witch's Cramp and render her completely helpless. Her fingers closed around the handle of a plastic water pitcher, and she threw it at him without looking to see what it was. It struck the mattress and bounced harmlessly to the side.

The rapid slap of rubber soles against linoleum came from the hallway: someone had obviously heard the racket.

Cobalt lifted his lip and snarled at the open doorway. "My servants!" he hissed. "Not yet! You may not disturb me until I have disposed of this brat! This abomination—"

Cobalt stopped where he was, and an almost comical look of shock came over his face. His knobby hands went to his chest and he bent over abruptly. For a long, crazy second, he appeared to be bowing to Deegie. His legs wobbled; his knees buckled. There was the quietest of thumps when he fell to the floor. He landed with his head nearly in Deegie's lap and she watched the light leave his eyes as he drew a final, ragged breath.

She crouched behind the nightstand, half-covered by the torn bed curtain, and just as the nurses burst into Room 195 her father's arm slid out from under the bed, snapped its fingers, and disappeared in a rather clichéd puff of smoke.

When Deegie looked down, she couldn't see her legs again; she was invisible once more. She observed briefly as the medical personnel fought to restore life to Cobalt's still body. Then, resisting the urge to spit on the dead man, she left the room and ran, unseen, down the hallway. She burst through the rear exit doors at a dead run and didn't stop until she reached the far end of the back parking lot.

A low brick wall surrounded most of the lot, and she leaned against it, breathing hard. A strange effervescent tingle ran through her body, and she realized she was becoming visible again. From somewhere in a tree branch far above, a jay scolded her repeatedly. Just as she was about to begin the process of grieving for her father all over again, a hot puff of air swirled around her head and he whispered in her ear, "*He must have forgotten I'm already dead! Besides, it's hard to kill a demon. Go home, Bunny. I love you.*"

Deegie spun in a frantic circle with her madly hammering heart lodged in her throat. Her entire body broke out in goosebumps. "Daddy, where are you?" she cried. "Please don't go! Please come back!"

Her only reply was the wind as it combed through the trees and cooled the tears running down her cheeks.

When she made it back to the motel room, the bag was still on the nightstand where she'd left it. She poked at it and dabbed her runny nose with a scratchy motel tissue. "Any chance of a quick trip home in there?" she asked aloud. But of course there was! The cell phone! She just needed to enter a code to open a portal home! She undid the bag's clasp, and her hand plunged inside, searching eagerly.

But the phone wasn't there.

"Oh hell no..." There was nothing left in the bag but a half-dozen twenties, folded in half and secured with the money clip. Deegie remembered the fast-food meal from last night and how it had simply appeared as soon as she'd thought of it. She clasped the bag to her chest and her pale brow furrowed. "I *need* that cell phone!" she said, and looked inside again. Just the money and the end of a drinking straw wrapper. The heavy rose-print fabric looked old and tired; it exuded a faint thrift-shop smell. The spell had been broken. It was just an ordinary bag now. She threw it down on the bed and patted all four pockets of her jeans again and again. Nothing. It must have fallen from her pocket during her harrowing adventure.

"Shit," Deegie said mildly. She picked up the bag and dusted it off. There was more than enough money for a cab ride home, but she was exhausted and longed for home; a portal would have made things so much easier. At least her father was still alive. Well, whatever passed for living in his world.

"Nothing should be easy, right, Dad?" she whispered the words as she inspected her face for damage in the fly-specked mirror. "I remember when you used to tell me that."

One of Cobalt's fire bolts had singed off a quarter-sized clump of her hair at the roots, and her shoulder throbbed dreadfully. She could just imagine the myriad of colors the bruise would display. Her head complained, too. She hovered on the edge of an attack of Witch's Cramp.

She saw the reflection of the bed in the mirror. It looked comfortable and inviting in spite of the rough, bleach-scented sheets. The room was paid up for another few hours. A hot shower would be bliss. She imagined she would use up the entire matchbook-sized bar of motel soap before she felt clean again. Perhaps a quick nap next. Home could wait for another hour or two. Maybe she could call Zach with the room's phone before her nap so he wouldn't worry.

Something thumped against the door.

Deegie jumped, a scream lodged in her throat.

The door shimmered from mid-point down, and something vague and indistinct moved across the carpet with a guttural *hngh, hngh, hngh.*

The tension left Deegie's body in a rush, and her body went limp with relief. *"Tiger!"* Her voice wavered and broke as she ran to embrace her old friend.

The mattress squawked and flattened as Tiger leaped onto the bed. Deegie lay down next to him, her call to Zach forgotten. Knowing that Tiger was on guard and at her side once again, she surrendered to sleep's insistent call.

Zach glared back at the balefully grinning insect-thing. "Come on, asshole," he muttered, tightening his hands into fists. "Come on in and see what you get!"

Keeping one eye on the flying monstrosity, Zach turned his head just enough to toss his shout over his shoulder, "Guys! They're coming in over here!"

Shrill cackles bubbled from the creature's tiny mouth, and it gave the cardboard another yank. The hole widened. Then the insect-creature twitched. Its grip loosened on the ragged cardboard and the creature dropped from the window. It fell, lifeless, into the snow. The rest of the swarm followed suit. Hundreds of dead insect-people plummeted to the ground.

The sun escaped from a bank of clouds. As its rays hit the fallen bodies, they began to sizzle and pop. Ribbons of acrid steam rose up to a stark blue sky and were borne away on the breeze. High in the branches of the closest tree, a bird uttered a cautious chirp.

"I think they got him," Zach said. He wiped the sweat from his face. Relief and a sense of triumph made his knees wobble. "They took out Cobalt. I think it's over."

CHAPTER FIFTEEN

Waking up was like clawing her way to the surface of a deep pool. She awoke in stages, first becoming aware that she had been dreaming. Cobalt's strange death had replayed itself in her mind, over and over, like it was stuck in a loop. The manic shrieking of decaying birds provided the background music. Something huge and warm was pressed against her, and sweat meandered down her neck in thin ribbons.

Deegie opened her eyes. Tiger was there next to her, his weight compressing the mattress to less than half its usual thickness. A faint smile curved her lips, and she closed her eyes again and snuggled closer to her invisible guardian.

A second later, she realized where she still was. She sprang from the bed, dazed and groggy. She hadn't meant to sleep so long; she should be home right now. She snatched up the phone receiver and her fingers were surprisingly quick on the key pad as she called for a taxi, telling them she'd be waiting in the parking lot. The room was stuffy and hot; she wanted out.

There was a timid knock on the door, followed by a muffled voice: "Housekeeping? Hello?"

"Just a minute!" Deegie called back. "Leaving right now!"

She found her coat and slid her feet into her boots. Her stomach grumbled unhappily, and an image of pancakes and sausage flashed through her head. She looked hopefully at the battered canvas bag, but when she opened it, there still wasn't anything inside but the money and that faint thrift shop smell. She picked it up and tucked it under her arm. It would make a good purse, anyway. "Come on Tiger," she whispered. "Let's go home."

The housekeeper was still waiting outside when Deegie opened the door. Arms crossed over her chest, she stood in front of her cart full of linens and cleaning implements. Her smile blinked on and off. Tiger grunted and his passing bulk shoved the cart against the pink stucco wall. The housekeeper scuttled backwards, both hands clapped to her mouth.

"Must have been a freak gust of wind," Deegie muttered. "Excuse me."

Having an eight-hundred-pound invisible tiger as a bodyguard had its challenges, but Deegie was grateful that Tiger was still with her. Still, he would need to return to the Spirit World during the cab ride home. There was no way Tiger would fit into the backseat of a taxi.

A row of vending machines stood along the wall next to the office: two for soda and one for snacks. Her stomach grumbled a gentle hint, and she rummaged in her pockets once more, in search of loose coins. As she perused the selections of salty, fatty snacks, the door to one of the rooms banged open, and two horrendously inebriated young men stumbled out. They headed in her direction. Their drunken guffaws echoed across the parking lot. "Hey!" one of them called out to her, "ya gettin' some candy? We like candy too!"

"Great," Deegie muttered under her breath. "Just what I needed right now, a couple of drunken idiots."

They weaved their way over to the vending machines and stood next to her, their boozy grins wide and eager. Happy hour had obviously started early for these two.

"Hey, Goth girl." The dark-haired one sidled up next to her. "Got some candy for us?"

Annoyed, she scowled at the two drunks and fed coins into the snack machine without replying. Tiger was still near, watching, protecting. Deegie wasn't afraid. She pressed a button at random. A bag of chips dropped from its peg, and she shoved it into the canvas bag.

"I don't think she talks, dude," the dark-haired one said to his friend. He leaned closer to Deegie. Sour beer breath wafted up her nose.

The blonde drunk cracked up. "Dude, sometimes it's better if chicks don't talk," he proclaimed. He reached out and flicked a finger against Deegie's curls. "Boing, boing, boing!" He snorted laughter through his nose and leaned against his friend to steady himself. "You got some biiiig boobies, too! Ya wanna party with us, goth girl?"

Deegie smirked as she watched the air ripple, mirage-like, behind the two party boys; Tiger was creeping up on them, ready to pounce and punish. She swatted Blondie's hand away from her hair. "Not interested," she said. "You might want to watch your back, though. There's a gigantic invisible tiger stalking you."

Their glazed eyes widened; their mouths dropped open, first one, then the other. "Dude!" Blondie hooted, "I think she's got the *good* stuff! Pass that shit over here, Gothy. We wanna check out the invisible tiger too!" He reached for her chest.

Deegie sidestepped and readied her casting hand. "So, you like boobs, huh?" She twisted her mouth into a tight, bitter smile. "You think big boobs are hot?"

"Hell yes!" Dark Hair's mouth was a wide, slobbering O.

"All right then," Deegie said. She pointed to Dark Hair, then to Blondie. "You want some boobs? Well, here you go!"

With a cry of *"Gynecomastia!"* she hurled a fast ball of red light at the two party boys. The parking lot lit up in a brief, brilliant flash of crimson.

It took several seconds for Blondie and Dark Hair to notice their new voluptuous curves, but when they did, all the mirth drained from their faces. Blondie ran his hand over his transformed anatomy and stared, horrified, at Deegie.

"Boobs! I have boobs! They won't come off! What is this fuckery?"

Dark Hair slapped at his newly enhanced chest and squawked, "Dude! Dude!" over and over.

Deegie winked. "Watch out for that invisible tiger!" she said.

Tiger bellowed, a thunderous roar that reverberated throughout the property. Deegie was sure she heard a touch of laughter in that roar.

The party boys, panic-stricken, wheeled around and scrambled back to their room. Their horrified shrieks were shrill and girlish. A few doors cracked open; startled faces peered out into the early evening gloom. "Hey!" someone shouted. "Shut the hell up!"

Tiger brushed against Deegie's legs, almost knocking her off-balance. His breath was warm, moist, and odious against her leg. It smelled like the bottom of a diaper pail, which wasn't unusual for him. Deegie shifted around. "Ew, Tiger. What did you eat? Come on now, chill out. They're gone."

He grunted and faded back, but not much. Deegie sensed him lurking around the perimeter of the parking lot. She heard the snuffle and huff of his sensitive nose as it sampled the air around the party boys' door.

Little jerks, she thought. *They deserve it. Damn it, where is that taxi?*

She yanked the strap of the musty canvas bag over her shoulder, then crossed both arms over her chest. Temperature and daylight were dropping fast. She could see her breath. Headlights cut across the parking lot: the cab, most likely. "Tiger," Deegie whispered, "go back to the Spirit World. You can't ride in the cab with me. I'm safe now."

Except it wasn't a cab. The vehicle pulling up beside her was a light blue pick-up with Altman Heating and Air painted on the doors. A man with shaggy red hair and a rust-colored beard sat at the wheel.

"Zach?" An enormous wave of relief weakened Deegie's knees. Zach leaned across the seat and opened the passenger side door. Deegie scrambled inside.

"Zach! Oh thank all the gods!" She slid across the seat and threw her arms around him. "I've never been so glad to see someone in my life. How did you find me?"

"Flower did. She's psychic or something. She said she had a vision of this motel, and—oh hell, I don't know. I'm just glad you're alive." Zach's voice was in her ear, his hands buried in her hair. "God, I was so worried about you!" Gently, he lifted her head away from his chest and ran his eyes over her face, as if he was looking for damage. "What happened to your hair? Are you all right, Deeg? You okay?"

"Yes, yes, just get me the hell out of here, okay?" She clung to him again. His wool shirt felt rough against her cheek, and she heard the thumping of his heart under her ear.

The truck shuddered and the cab lifted upwards slightly, as if a great weight had been dumped in the back. The springs creaked and groaned.

"What the hell's wrong with my—" Zach braced himself against the dashboard, and a look of disgust passed over his face. "—And what is that *smell?*"

"It's Tiger," Deegie said. "He won't go back to the Spirit World until he's sure I'm safe." She slid open the cab's back window, turned around in her seat, and murmured to what appeared to be an empty truck bed. The truck's springs squawked again, and the vehicle righted itself.

"He's gone back," Deegie said. "For now, anyway." She faced front and buckled her seat belt. "Take me home now, Zach. It's over. We won."

Once they were back on the road with the motel getting smaller and smaller in the rear-view mirror, Zach filled Deegie in on the events that had taken place at her house during her absence. He told her of the insect people with their dripping, venomous stings, and the way they had poured down the chimney and into the fire; the brief, victorious battle—and the tragic demise of Mike Rosenstraum. She listened quietly, eyes closed, hands folded into one another.

"I feel like it's my fault, Zach," she said softly. "People died because of me. I wish I'd never told anyone what was happening." Headlights from passing cars spotlighted her wan face and deepened the dark crescents under her eyes at the same time.

"Don't... don't think like that, Deeg," Zach said. He cleared his throat and swallowed hard. "It's not like you forced anyone to help; they wanted to. Cobalt is—was—a bad dude. You and your dad put a stop to any more suffering. You did a *good* thing, a *brave* thing. Nobody's blaming you. Okay?"

Deegie nodded, but her expression did not change. "He tried to kill my dad. Stupid man. My dad's already dead. Cobalt died on his own, by the way. Heart attack or something. I never got a chance to... to..." She swallowed the rest of her sentence; it didn't matter anymore. "Enough of that," she said. "It's over." Her stomach grumbled unhappily, and she winced and pressed her hands against her abdomen.

"It's over," Zach echoed her words. "Everything's okay now. You're safe, and that's all that matters to me." He took his eyes off the road just long enough to glance over at Deegie. "And when was the last time you had something to eat?"

"Um... I dunno. Yesterday, I think."

"Feel like stopping at Dos Hombres? We could have nachos again, like we did on our date a while back. Remember? You got to meet Shit Storm Murphy then."

Deegie managed a smile. "That was a date?"

"Oh, well, maybe it wasn't a date, then," Zach stammered. "I just thought you might like to—"

Deegie chuckled softly and opened her eyes. "I'm kidding, you big goof," she said. "Yes, nachos sound fantastic right now." She reached over and patted his arm. "And it can be a date if you want it to be," she added, surprising herself.

In the Dos Hombres parking lot, Deegie unbuckled her seat belt, scooted across the seat, and wrapped her arms around Zach again. "Thank you," she said. "Thank you for coming to get me. Thank you for fighting for me, and thank you for putting up with my crap. You're such a good friend."

Awkwardly, he hugged her back, then pulled away to look at her. "You don't have to thank me," he told her. "I'm happy to put up with your crap. I love you, don't you know that?"

"What? You do?" The growling in her belly was replaced with an odd fluttering sensation. A flush rose from her neck all the way into her hairline. "You mean like… like friends love each other, or…?"

Zach shook his head and tightened his arms around her again. "No," he said. "I mean I *love* you. Haven't you figured that out yet?"

"Well, I don't know, I mean—I guess so, but I…" Her heart somersaulted in her chest, and she tried again. "Okay," she said. "I can handle that. That's cool. I guess I just never…"

Zach laughed. "Just shut up so I can kiss you," he said, and he put his mouth over hers before she could say anything else.

It was the gurgling of Deegie's stomach that interrupted them. If she hadn't been so hungry, she would have gladly stayed in the cab of Zach's work truck for the rest of the night. She pulled away from him with an embarrassed chuckle. "Sorry," she said. "I didn't mean to spoil the moment."

"I thought Tiger was in here for a minute," Zach said with a wink. "And there will be plenty of other moments for us—if you want them, that is."

"Of course I do, Zach. I just… I'm not very good at this." She offered a weak shrug and an uncharacteristically bashful smile. She wiped damp palms against her pant legs, opened her mouth to say something else, then gave up and returned to his arms.

"You're silly," said Zach. He lifted her chin with a fingertip and kissed the end of her nose. "Come on, let's feed you and get you home. Bast misses you, and Gilbert probably needs to be yelled at."

———◆———

With the help of the Altman brothers and her new friends, Deegie's old house was put in order once more. New glass was put in the windows, the living room was repainted, and the gore-splattered patchwork couch was replaced with a purple pleather loveseat and recliner that Deegie liked even better. Soon the house was neat, clean, and in even better shape than it had been in before. The only reminder of the Great Witch War of Fiddlehead Creek was an occasional nightmare, but Deegie knew those would eventually fade.

The weather showed signs of an early spring. The snow melted steadily, revealing large muddy patches in the back yard. Tender blades of new grass emerged and took advantage of the sun's generosity. Deegie spent a considerable amount of time online, researching lawn and rosebush care and deciding which types of roses to plant over Lisbet's resting spot.

As for Lisbet herself, the timid ghost had sequestered herself in the attic with her spectral cats and would only come down if Deegie was alone in the house. Her beautiful soprano voice no longer echoed through the house, and she had ceased her cheerful giggle. Deegie tried her best to convince her friend that all was well now, and all the "bad things" were gone, but to no avail. She didn't blame Lisbet, though; there had been far too many horrible things happening in this house. If it were possible for a ghost to be traumatized, then Lisbet certainly was. Deegie could only hope that it would soon pass.

On a cold, clear morning in mid-March, Deegie and Flower were preparing one of the downstairs bedrooms for the homeless cats that Deegie hoped to be fostering soon. Bast lounged in the sunny windowsill, overseeing the job and taking particular interest in the multi-level cat tower the women were putting together. Deegie and Flower had formed an immediate bond; the older woman reminded Deegie of her own mother, and it was good to have another female to confide in. Flower loved cats as well, and she was almost as excited about the cat sanctuary as Deegie was.

"I might have to ask the guys for help when we start screening off the back porch," Deegie said to her new friend as she fitted the top of the cat tower in place. "I'd probably wind up staple-gunning my hand to the wall or something."

Flower chuckled and tossed her long gray hair over her shoulder. "You and me both," she said. "I'm completely inept when it comes to tools. Too bad there isn't a spell for screening off a porch!" She patted Deegie's cheek and studied her face. "Feeling okay, honey?" she asked. "Your mouth is smiling, but your eyes are so sad."

"Yeah, I'm okay," Deegie said, and she nodded with an enthusiasm she didn't really feel. "I'm just a little tired, that's all."

While Deegie was fine physically, it would be a while before her head felt normal again. The horror was over, and Cobalt was dead, but her mind insisted on replaying certain parts of her latest misadventure. Mostly it was images of her father, or, more accurately, the demonic being her father had become. When she closed her eyes, she could still see his serrated teeth and his flashing, opalescent eyes. He was alive, yet not alive; evil, yet good. She would have given anything to see him again, preferably under better circumstances.

Deegie changed the subject before Flower could press the issue. "Looks like Gilbert and Nix are spending a lot of time together," she said, putting an extra brightness into her smile.

"I've noticed that too. They make a good couple. Both of them are just as stubborn as mules." Flower cocked an eyebrow at Deegie and added, "And how are you and Zach getting along? You two have been thick as thieves lately."

"Zach's a great guy," Deegie said. "I think… I think we will be good together. He understands me, and he likes cats."

Flower nodded, but her expression darkened. "Mike Rosenstraum liked cats too," she said. "And I liked him. I miss him."

Deegie's throat tightened, and she swallowed hard. "I'm… I'm so sorry," she said. "I didn't know that—"

"Sh, don't fuss, Deegie. He and Danny Q. were good men. They were heroes." Flower picked up Bast and nuzzled his sun-warmed fur. "Let's focus on the happy things that are happening now, okay?" Tears glimmered in her eyes; Deegie had to look away.

The front door banged open, and familiar footsteps clomped across the floor: Zach had returned from the hardware store with the cans of latex paint Deegie needed. "I'll be right back," she said. "I'd better go make sure he got the right paint. You know how guys are."

"You go right ahead," the older witch replied. "Bast and I can finish up here."

Deegie met Zach in the kitchen; the paint cans were on the table, awaiting her approval. She ignored them and hugged Zach instead, breathing in his comforting coffee and shaving cream scent. "Thanks," she said, "that was fast!"

"I missed you," Zach replied, his lips against her neck. "Had to haul ass and get back here."

"You're a dork." She gave him a quick peck on the lips. "Did you remember the paint roller and the brushes?"

"Yep, and I ordered the chicken wire for the porch. Got these for you, too." He delved into the pocket of his denim jacket and took out a variety of candy bars. "I thought maybe I could help you eat them, you know, later on." His cheeks pinkened and he winked at her. "Chocolate tastes best under a down comforter, so I've been told."

Deegie snickered and undid the top button of his shirt. "Oh really? And what's that supposed to mean, Mr. Altman?"

A sudden puff of cool air swirled around the two of them before Zach could reply, and something misty and gray appeared next to the table. Indistinct at first, the gray mist undulated and shimmered, and finally coalesced into the shape of a tiny, plump woman with a long silver braid: Lisbet.

"Lisbet!" Deegie gasped excitedly. "You came down! I'm so glad!"

Lisbet smiled at Deegie. She drifted closer and stood next to Zach, looking him up and down, then she touched his arm with a transparent finger. Goosebumps rose on his skin.

"Hi, Lisbet." Zach's voice was a hesitant whisper, as if he was afraid of frightening her away. "It's… it's nice to see you."

"*Good, good…*" Lisbet said. She turned to Deegie and beamed. "*Nice to see… nice to see. Was worried, me. Was worried you would choose the brother instead.*" Her bright eyes twinkled and her good hand rose to her mouth to stifle a giggle. "*Happy for love,*" she said. "*So happy for new love.*"

Epilogue

Tamara Biggs didn't normally steal things, but the woman in the magic shop had really pissed her off, and she figured she had a right to help herself. Maybe casting a love spell on her classmate, Mitch Timmons, really *wasn't* a good idea, but the shop owner didn't have to be such a bitch about it. According to her parents, one of Tamara's ancestors had been executed for practicing witchcraft during that Salem witch hunt thing in the late sixteen hundreds. *Too bad she's not here now,* Tamara thought. *I bet she would cast a love spell for me. And she was a real witch, not like that poser at The Silent Cat. And I bet she'd be cool to hang out with, too. Unlike this preachy, church-going family of mine. Anyway, what's done is done. Too late now.*

Tamara slid the purloined item out from under her bed and had another look at it. *What exactly is this thing?* she wondered as she took it out of the plastic shopping bag she'd stored it in. It looked a little like the ubiquitous Ouija Board, but it was round, in a faded orange hue, and looked quite old. *Maybe it's worth some money,* she thought, running her fingers over the elaborate gold leaf alphabet around the edges. *Maybe I can sell it and get some weed instead.*

She heard her parents and little brother bustling about and making their "getting ready for church" noises. Pretty soon they would be pounding on her door, asking her if she was ready to go too. Time to fake another illness; going to church was so damn boring. Tamara slipped the talking board back into the bag and shoved it under the bed just as the anticipated knock sounded on her bedroom door. She dove beneath the covers and affected a weak, whispery voice:

"Mama? That you…?"

The door opened and her mother stood there, hands on hips and looking thoroughly annoyed. "Don't tell me, let me guess—you're sick again, aren't you?"

"Cramps, Mama. Can't help it. I can't go to church in this condition."

Her mother's sigh sounded pained and she gazed heavenward for a second before replying. "Alright, Tamara. I guess I can't argue with that. Just remember, though—He's watching you!" She pointed upwards to give her daughter a hint as to whom she meant.

"Yes, Mama." Tamara was pissing herself off now; she sounded exactly like that Carrie girl from that freaky movie.

Her mother hauled her purse strap over her shoulder and turned to go. "Your eighteenth birthday party is in two days, but I'm sure you'll be just fine for that, won't you?"

"Yes, Mama."

Her mother muttered something unintelligible and closed the door with more force than necessary.

Tamara listened as the family station wagon pulled out of the driveway and down Clover Street. When she could no longer hear the engine, she threw back the covers and retrieved the talking board from under the bed. A few minutes' worth of research on her laptop told her that this thing was worth at least two hundred dollars, more than enough for some quality smoke if she could find someone to buy it. But first she wanted to try it out just to see if it worked. Who knows, maybe it told fortunes or something. She snatched up her cell phone from the bedside table and dialed her best friend and partner in crime, Tiffany Kunis.

"Tiff? Yeah, it's me. I got out of it again, of course. Total waste of time, if you ask me. Hey, do you feel like having a sleepover? I just got this cool fortune-telling thing, but I don't know how it works. Wanna help me figure it out?"

To be continued...

BONUS CHAPTER: DEEGIE'S RECIPES

I'm pleased to share some more of Deegie's recipes with you. Well, actually they're *my* recipes, but I let her think they're hers. Enjoy!

HERBAL TEAS FOR COLDS AND FLU

My poor little Deegie is so sick at the beginning of this book! I like to think she brewed up a pot or two of these wonderfully soothing herbal teas. It's always best to use organic ingredients whenever possible.

COLD AND FLU TEA VERSION #1
1 tablespoon dried sage leaves
1 tablespoon catnip (yes, catnip!)
1 tablespoon dried peppermint leaves
1 quart spring water
Juice of one lemon
Honey to taste.

Place dried herbs in a large heatproof bowl. Bring water to a boil and pour over the herbs. Let steep for fifteen minutes, strain, and add lemon juice. Sweeten to taste with honey.

Sage, honey, and lemon juice have antiseptic properties, and peppermint helps with congestion. Catnip is a mild sleep-inducer, is good for headaches, and contains vitamins C and E.

Important: It is always a good idea to consult with your doctor or healer before using herbal remedies, as they can react with certain medications. Pregnant women should not use catnip as it can stimulate menstruation.

COLD AND FLU TEA VERSION #2
¼ cup dried lemon balm leaves
2 tablespoons ground fennel seed
1 quart spring water
Juice of one lemon
Honey to taste

Brew as for Version # 1 (above). Lemon balm helps bring on a sweat that is good for relieving colds and flu, and it also contains an anti-viral agent. Fennel is good for respiratory issues, and helps with sore throat and coughing.

Important: It is always a good idea to consult with your doctor or healer before using herbal remedies as they can react with certain medications.

ROSE PETAL JELLY
(Jelly-making skills are required for this one!)
4 to 5 cups organic, washed rose petals
2 teaspoons chamomile buds
½ teaspoon lavender buds
3½ cups boiling water
1 package pectin
4 cups organic, unrefined cane sugar
Canning jars

Place rose petals, lavender, and chamomile into a bowl and pour in the boiling water. Cover and let it steep for an hour. Strain the liquid into a stainless steel pot and discard the herbs. Add the pectin to the liquid, bring to a boil, and add sugar all at once. Bring mixture to a rolling boil, stirring constantly, then boil for one minute. Remove from heat, skim off foam, then pour into sterilized, hot jars, and seal. Makes about five cups.

SPICED WINE

(non-alcoholic version)

4 teaspoons cinnamon

4 teaspoons ginger

2-inch piece of vanilla bean

3 cups red grape juice

With a sharp knife, make a series of shallow cuts along the length of the vanilla bean to release its essence. Place grape juice in a pitcher or bowl, and add the herbs and vanilla bean. Cover and place in refrigerator for a couple of days, then strain and serve. For the alcoholic version, replace the grape juice with three cups of red wine.

PET PROTECTION CHARMS

Brown felt or other cloth

Brown thread and a sewing needle

A bit of dried cedar (you can use the cedar shavings for small animal cages)

A few hairs from your pet (go check the couch)

1 dried bay leaf

A few black peppercorns

A few pinches of catnip (no matter what kind of pet you have)

Cut two 2-inch circles from the brown fabric and sew them together with the needle and thread, leaving a small opening. Stuff the pouch with the rest of the ingredients and sew it firmly closed. If you wish, you can write or embroider your pet's name on the pouch. Hang it near your pet's bed and take it in the car with you when you take your pet for rides. You can also hang it from your pet's collar, but make sure they don't mind first, and be sure the pouch is sewn tightly shut and securely attached to the pet's collar.

WEREWOLF PROTECTION CHARMS

(because hey, you never know!)

Black felt or other cloth

Black thread and a sewing needle

A hefty pinch of dried marigold petals, or wolfsbane, if you can find it

A small piece of silver, like a ring or a coin

A small piece of hematite or tiger's eye gemstone

Cut two 2-inch circles from the black fabric, and sew them together with the needle and thread, leaving a small opening. Stuff the pouch with the rest of the ingredients and sew closed. Write your initials on it if you like. Carry it with you during the full moon—just in case!

COCONUT AND HONEY FACIAL CLEANSER

¼ cup organic, unrefined coconut oil

¼ cup of raw, unfiltered honey

Put the coconut oil and honey in a saucepan over gentle heat and stir until the mixture is warm and thoroughly mixed. Massage mixture over your face and rinse thoroughly with warm water. Store covered in the fridge. If the cleanser solidifies, just place the container in a bowl of hot water until it liquefies. This stuff makes a great make-up remover, and coconut oil and honey have moisturizing and anti-bacterial qualities, making it perfect for zits *and* wrinkles!

ABOUT THE AUTHOR

C.L. Hernandez is an author of fiction, horror, and dark fantasy. She has been writing since she was very young, but never gave a thought to being published until 2012. In 2014, she self-published two short story collections, *Cobwebs* and *A Half-Dozen Horrors*, and a short, true-life ghost story called *A Woman's Touch*. In addition to writing, she enjoys crocheting and a variety of crafts. She lives in California's Central Valley with her daughter, Olivia, two cats, and a turtle named George.

PERMUTED
PRESS
needs **you** to help

SPREAD (THE) INFECTION

FOLLOW US!

f | Facebook.com/PermutedPress
🐦 | Twitter.com/PermutedPress

REVIEW US!

Wherever you buy our book, they can be reviewed! We want to know what you like!

GET INFECTED!

Sign up for our mailing list at PermutedPress.com

PERMUTED
PRESS

KING ARTHUR AND THE KNIGHTS OF THE ROUND TABLE HAVE BEEN REBORN TO SAVE THE WORLD FROM THE CLUTCHES OF MORGANA WHILE SHE PROPELS OUR MODERN WORLD INTO THE MIDDLE AGES.

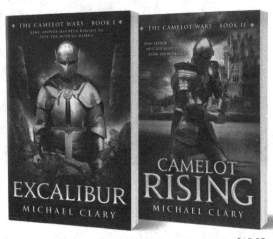

EAN 9781618685018 $15.99   EAN 9781682611562 $15.99

Morgana's first attack came in a red fog that wiped out all modern technology. The entire planet was pushed back into the middle ages. The world descended into chaos.

But hope is not yet lost— King Arthur, Merlin, and the Knights of the Round Table have been reborn.

THE ULTIMATE PREPPER'S ADVENTURE.
THE JOURNEY BEGINS HERE!

EAN 9781682611654 $9.99   EAN 9781618687371 $9.99   EAN 9781618687395 $9.99

The long-predicted Coronal Mass Ejection has finally hit the Earth, virtually destroying civilization. Nathan Owens has been prepping for a disaster like this for years, but now he's a thousand miles away from his family and his refuge. He'll have to employ all his hard-won survivalist skills to save his current community, before he begins his long journey through doomsday to get back home.

THE MORNINGSTAR STRAIN HAS BEEN LET LOOSE—IS THERE ANY WAY TO STOP IT?

An industrial accident unleashes some of the Morningstar Strain. The

EAN 9781618686497 $16.00

doctor who discovered the strain and her assistant will have to fight their way through Sprinters and Shamblers to save themselves, the vaccine, and the base. Then they discover that it wasn't an accident at all—somebody inside the facility did it on purpose. The war with the RSA and the infected is far from over.

This is the fourth book in Z.A. Recht's The Morningstar Strain series, written by Brad Munson.

PERMUTED
PRESS

GATHERED TOGETHER AT LAST, THREE TALES OF FANTASY CENTERING AROUND THE MYSTERIOUS CITY OF SHADOWS...ALSO KNOWN AS CHICAGO.

EAN 9781682612286 $9.99   **EAN** 9781618684639 $5.99   **EAN** 9781618684899 $5.99

From *The New York Times* and *USA Today* bestselling author Richard A. Knaak comes three tales from Chicago, the City of Shadows. Enter the world of the Grey–the creatures that live at the edge of our imagination and seek to be real. Follow the quest of a wizard seeking escape from the centuries-long haunting of a gargoyle. Behold the coming of the end of the world as the Dutchman arrives.

Enter the City of Shadows.

PERMUTED
PRESS

WE CAN'T GUARANTEE THIS GUIDE WILL SAVE YOUR LIFE. BUT WE CAN GUARANTEE IT WILL KEEP YOU SMILING WHILE THE LIVING DEAD ARE CHOWING DOWN ON YOU.

EAN 9781618686695 $9.99

This is the only tool you need to survive the zombie apocalypse.

OK, that's not really true. But when the SHTF, you're going to want a survival guide that's not just geared toward day-to-day survival. You'll need one that addresses the essential skills for true nourishment of the human spirit. Living through the end of the world isn't worth a damn unless you can enjoy yourself in any way you want. (Except, of course, for anything having to do with abuse. We could never condone such things. At least the publisher's lawyers say we can't.)